MHardulé

RAVES FOR *BONITA FAYE*

"Bonita Faye is the Eliza Doolittle of the dustbowl."
—Associated Press

"Delightful … Memorable … [Bonita Faye's] poignant, humorous and always insightful account of life and death and their effects on the soul are captivating.… Best of all, this author offers a startling fresh voice and a literary original you'll want to share with friends."
—*Tulsa World*

"Absolute living proof that the toughest women in the world are Southern."
—*Fort Worth Star-Telegram*

"Kept me up all night. She has more warmth, wit and human insight than any fictional character I've read since Fanny Flagg's *Fried Green Tomatoes*, which was a delight in both book and movie versions. Margaret Moseley's first novel is a real page-turner and deserves equal success."
—*Southwest Times Record*
(Fort Smith, Arkansas)

"Moseley's crisp style carries the reader quickly to a powerful and unexpected ending."
—*Fort Worth Weekly*

"Her humor is priceless a[nd] Faye Burnett."
—

BONITA FAYE

MARGARET MOSELEY

HarperPaperbacks
A Division of HarperCollins*Publishers*

HarperPaperbacks
A Division of HarperCollins*Publishers*
10 East 53rd Street, New York, N.Y. 10022-5299

This is a work of fiction. The characters, incidents, and dialogues are products of the author's imagination and are not to be construed as real. Any resemblance to actual events or persons, living or dead, is entirely coincidental.

ISBN 0-06-101189-4

HarperCollins®, ■®, and HarperPaperbacks™ are trademarks of HarperCollins*Publishers*, Inc.

A hardcover edition of this book was published in 1996 by Three Forks Press

Cover illustration by Christopher O'Leary

First HarperPaperbacks printing: May 1997

Printed in the United States of America

Visit HarperPaperbacks on the World Wide Web at http://www.harpercollins.com/paperbacks

❖ 10 9 8 7 6 5 4 3 2

For Dixie and Charlotte

ACKNOWLEDGMENTS

To acknowledge support is one thing . . . to acknowledge the love that goes with the support . . . another. I have both . . . and therein am blessed. . . . Mary Lou and Donna. Cassey, Frances, and my Annie. And Darwin, Greg and Carolyn.

Along the way . . . The Bluestocking Book Club . . . and the FSLT gang.

Along the cyber way . . . MikeComb, BobbyWrite, RonBurris, Soul, Chazwrite, Robert873, Kairos8, Phylwriter and THopeB, Tom Clancy, Restless34, PRLG, AuthorDB, and all the others in the Writer's Club who said . . . "Go for it, Marigo . . ."

And especially to Dawn . . . whose spirit of survival . . . is equal to that of Bonita Faye!

ONE

It was only a little murder. He wasn't even an important man. And it happened so long ago—forty years ago to be exact. That's why I don't understand why everyone got so upset. If anyone shoulda been shocked, it shoulda been me. After all I was married to him.

You can't tell by looking at me now, but I was a little, bitty thing back then. Not bigger than a minute. Why, when I look down at this stranger's body I carry around now, I wonder if I really am the same young girl who married Billy Roy Burnett in 1949.

Don't that seem long ago? Why, that was ten years before they even opened the Black Angus Cafe and it seems like that cafe has been there on the highway forever. Can you imagine Poteau without the Angus? Where would the people eat on Sundays after church? Where would the Lions meet? Why, there wouldn't be no town at all without the Angus.

It weren't there in 1950 either when Billy Roy died. I don't like saying "murdered." Do you?

Just think. If there'd been a Black Angus Cafe back

then, that's where I would of been when Harmon came to tell me about Billy Roy. Instead, I was at home frying Sunday dinner chicken when he came. We always had fried chicken after church and even though Billy Roy wasn't home, I was frying away like always. Like he'd be coming in any minute, atelling me where he'd been and why he'd missed coming home last night.

So when the knock sounded at the front door, I jumped a tad. Billy Roy would have just slammed on in through the kitchen door. Guess I was thinking about that and that's what startled me when Harmon knocked at the front.

I went to the door with a pink apron over my go-to-meeting clothes. I know I should have changed before I started cooking, but you can see nothing about that day seemed right anyway. So, there I was, with flour from the chicken all over my apron, and some on my nose, when I opened the door.

I saw that it was Harmon through the oval glass in the door. We didn't have many fancy things back in those days and I took a lot of pride in that etched glass in the front door. Always made sure there was a light burning in the hall at night, so everybody passing by could see how it shone so clear. Didn't care how much Billy Roy razzed.

I had never met Harmon, but I had heard him talk once at a town meeting back when they was trying to make the Heavener Runestone a state park. Harmon was a state trooper then, the best looking one Oklahoma had ever seen, and he was going on in his speech about how if all of us town folk got behind the park, just a few miles from Poteau, it would attract tourism and we'd all be rich as Mr. Got Rocks himself. I didn't pay much mind to his words, but he sure was handsome in his starched brown uniform.

That's really what I saw first through the glass, the brown uniform. It was when I opened the door, that I saw Harmon in it.

He sure was excited and some embarrassed when he started talking. "Mrs. Burnett? Mrs. Billy Roy Burnett?"

Well, of course, I said I was. Sometimes I rattle on, more now than what I used to, but that time I just stood silent as a stump and let him talk.

"Mrs. Burnett, I hate to be the one to tell you this, but your husband, Billy Roy, is dead." After getting it out, he just stared at me like I was staring at him.

It was like after the telling, there was no more to be said about the matter, but after a minute, it got uncomfortable so he started speaking again.

"He, Billy Roy, was up on the mountain." Everybody called Cavanal Hill a mountain, but legally it's nothing but the highest hill in the United States.

I decided to help him out. "Yes?"

Glad I was talking, he went on. "Your husband was shot, Mrs. Burnett. Murdered, it looks like. I sure am sorry to be the one to tell you this," he added again.

Harmon was still standing in the doorway, his back against the one o'clock sun that peeked out over his left shoulder. When I stared into that sun, all I could make out of him was a black silhouette. The glare in my eyes made them water and a tickling started in the back of my nose. I sneezed, but being polite I caught the sneeze in the hem of my apron. When I raised my face, all Harmon could see were my red teary eyes.

He said later, that was what prompted him to come on in the house and take me in his arms. "Oh, I'm so sorry, Mrs. Burnett. I ain't never done this before. I knew I'd get it wrong."

"Don't be silly," I said. I could smell the starch in his brown uniform as he held me in a comforting clutch. I wanted to tell him he was good at the consoling part, but I didn't tell him that until after we were married.

We just stood there in the hall and patted each other. My eyes were still running and all Harmon seemed to know to do was pat my back like he was burping a baby.

That's when I heard the sizzling of the chicken in the frying pan. I ran into the kitchen and Harmon followed.

While I was turning the chicken so it'd brown even, Harmon kept stammering on about Billy Roy. "Don't you worry none, Mrs. Burnett. We're going to catch whoever done this to you."

Nobody hadn't done nothing to me. I was the one standing in the kitchen, alive and cooking chicken. Billy Roy was the one who was dead. Besides no one had ever done anything for me in my life. Everything that had ever happened to me, I had made happen. Even marrying Billy Roy. Sometimes I didn't know what was good for me and what wasn't.

The chicken was done, perfect like I always make. I turned off the gas and stared at the golden chicken parts piled up on the blue platter. Harmon alternated, eyeing first me and then the plate. We were both young and didn't know what came next.

So we ate the chicken.

"Where is he? Billy Roy?" In case he had forgotten who had brought us together for this Sunday meal.

"They're bringing him into Wilson's—Sheriff Hoyle and the others. Don't reckon you'll want to be seeing him before Mr. Wilson gets to him. He wasn't pretty, Mrs. Burnett." Harmon and I did what we were getting good at. We stared at the chicken bone in Harmon's right hand. You could see the curved shape of Harmon's mouth where he had taken a bite out of the leg. Under the flaky crust, you could see the chicken meat, dark and shining with oil. Muscle and fat covered the tendons and veins of the exposed flesh and bone. Globules of fat burst from the still hot meat and a little slid down Harmon's thumb. He put the leg down and wiped it on the starched napkin I had given him when we sat down. The oil in the chicken made his thumbnail shine like he had a manicure.

I don't know how long we would have gone on sitting there, staring and eating. I don't know 'cause people started coming.

Ever notice how they do that?

They just start coming to the house of death just as sure as if there were a steeple over it with the bell tolling a message. "Someone's dead. Come one, come all. There's food to be had and kitchens to clean. Come one, come all. Do your part for the dead."

Years later, when we were older, my best friend Patsy and I made a pact. Whoever died first, the survivor would come and clean out the crumbs from the silverware drawer before the church ladies got there. You could have unmade beds and dust bunnies under the couch, but it was the silverware drawer crumbs that turned them on.

When Billy Roy died, I didn't know that. I took a glass of lemonade from Mrs. Pearleman and went out front to sit in the porch swing while the ones who came to comfort cleaned out my silverware drawer with whispered "tsks, tsks." I wasn't a dirty housekeeper, it was just that this was Sunday and silverware drawer cleaning wasn't until Monday.

They cleaned my house from kitchen to storage closet, inspecting anything in the closets or drawers they wanted to.

My real Paris nightgown got the most looks. I heard Martha Hannagen whisper to Ethel Stockman as they passed in the hall, "Third drawer on the left, behind the hose and under the blue tissue paper. Don't miss it."

Harmon left.

I didn't see him go, but the next brown uniform that stood in front of me was Sheriff Hoyle's.

"Mrs. Burnett, Mrs. Burnett." He sounded like he had been saying my name for a long time before I heard him.

"Mrs. Burnett, I want to tell you what we know. And I gotta ask you some questions." Sheriff Hoyle sounded apologetic about being intrusive into my grief.

Now I can imagine what kind of picture I must have presented to him. Sitting on one leg on the porch swing, the other dangling useless except when I pumped it forward with my body to move the swing in a slow motion. Black hair shining like a tight satin cap, big eyes, a slight waifish body in a blue dress ten years too old for the wearer. No makeup and a pale, pale complexion.

I was just too frail and vulnerable for him to stand, but he had to do his duty. So he did it gently.

"Mrs. Burnett, when did Billy Roy go up on the mountain?"

"Saturday mornin'."

"Did anyone go with him?"

"No."

"What was he doing up there?" I guess that was one of those "for the record" questions. Everybody knew why anyone went up on Cavanal Hill on a Saturday morning before deer season.

"When did you expect him back?"

This was the first interesting question. I turned my face up toward his. I hadn't invited him to share the swing with me and he was standing, asking questions in rhythm to my pumping. Asking when the swing was forward and scribbling in his notebook when it was away from him.

"Lord, I never know when to expect Billy Roy back, Sheriff Hoyle. When they're no more deer to shoot. When they're no more fish to catch. When he runs out of whiskey, worms, or gunshot."

"You weren't worried about him when he didn't come home last night?"

"No, I just read my books, went to bed and then got up this mornin' and went to church. You know that. You and Berta sat behind me." They had, too. Alike even to the left sided parts in their hair. Both in their gray serge suits. Shiny serge covered their vast abdomens and I could smell spot-cleaning fluid even over in my pew. Her suit had black grosgrain trim on the collar and sleeves. They had stood and sat together in the intimate rhythm of two people who have been together so long they anticipate and mime the other without conscious thought. Up and down they had got to sing and pray, each excursion sending out fresh wafts of Berta's home cleaning efforts.

Sheriff Hoyle musta changed into his uniform when somebody told him about Billy Roy. Berta was right now in my bedroom easing open the third drawer on the left. She still had on her serge.

"Bonita Faye, think carefully. Can you think of anyone who would want to kill Billy Roy?"

His calling me Bonita Faye instead of Mrs. Burnett surrounded the interrogation with a private atmosphere. And, of course, the least thing that smacked of private or confidential in Poteau was exactly what everyone wanted to know most.

The men, husbands of the cleaning ladies, were all lounged around the porch, mainly on the steps and banister. They had been gossiping and smoking while I was swinging. Ever so often one of them would glance my way; young widows being a novelty. But I never spoke to them when I was married, so we didn't have nothing to say now either.

The men suspended their conversations and turned in unison to hear my answer to Sheriff Hoyle.

I gave the swing an extra pump before I answered. "Why, no, Sheriff. Do you?"

TWO

I sat there swinging on that porch for hours. The sun and the town comforters had long since departed. Even my friend Patsy.

I had got up once to go to the bathroom, apologizing for bumping into the women parading through my house. The bathroom had been added on to the house years before and jutted off by itself down the hall near the door to the one bedroom. When I closed the door so I could use the toilet, I noticed someone had put out my good set of towels on the rack and washed off the spilled powder on the sink and put away my bobbypins.

When I lifted the toilet lid, I saw one of the housekeepers had managed to scrub the bowl clean of its perpetual rust stains. Wish I knew who had done it. It was bound to come back and if someone had a secret formula for cleaning rust out of toilet bowls, I wanted to know it.

I also sat at the kitchen table for a slice of Ethel's chocolate layer cake. I remember that. I just don't remember how I wound up back in the swing, watching the cars move out of the yard. It musta been twilight 'cause some cars had their lights on and some didn't.

I remember Patsy saying she'd stay with me, and then I musta said no in a rude way 'cause she looked hurt. She got over it though and brought me my white sweater to put on before she left to cross the field to her own house. The night was turning cool and the sweater felt good even though it was a bit scratchy.

Finally I was alone and could think. But, like me and Harmon had felt in the kitchen earlier, I didn't know what came next.

It was close to ten-thirty when I decided what to do. I came in the house, locked the door behind me and went into the kitchen to the telephone.

Miss Dorothy, the town telephone operator, librarian, and postmistress, answered on the fourth ring. When she recognized it was me, she had to tell me how sorry she was about Billy Roy and how sorry she was not to have come to the house to clean, but she had been on call at the switchboard all day. However, she was making me her pineapple upside-down cake. She remembered how much Billy Roy had liked it.

After all that, she gave me Harmon Adams's telephone number.

He answered on the first ring.

"Harmon, this is Bonita Faye Burnett."

"Yes, Bonita Faye, I mean, Mrs. Burnett. Hello. How are you?"

I didn't know if he was asking because he wanted to know or if it was just part of his telephone etiquette. Etiquette is always getting in the way of people getting down to what they really want to do or say.

"I'm fine." I knew my role lines, too.

Then I got down to it.

"Listen, Harmon. I want to go see the place where . . . where Billy Roy was murd . . . shot . . . killed. Where he died, I mean. I want to go there now."

"Now, now, Bonita Faye, you can't mean that." No more Mrs. Burnett, not now or ever again.

"Yes, I do, Harmon Adams. And I want you to take me. Come and get me in your truck." I know I sounded excited, maybe hysterical.

Harmon tried to dissuade me or at least, please, Bonita Faye, wait until tomorrow morning when it was light. It was only when I told him I was going to walk to Cavanal Hill by myself, right now, that he agreed to come pick me up.

I was waiting for him on the steps, hunkered down by the banister where the husbands had sat all afternoon. I ran toward the pickup in the dark just as soon as it slowed down in front of the house. In my big, longsleeved white sweater I musta looked like a ghost gliding across the lawn. I ran around the front of the truck and opened the door to jump in.

"Jesus, Bonita Faye, you coulda waited until I came to a full stop." Harmon's face was pale and green from the reflection of the light panel on the dashboard. He still had on his starched uniform, probably had put it on when I called, but in an indecisive gesture to the semi-officialness of this meeting, he had his collar open and one sleeve rolled up. What would a young police officer wear to take an attractive new widow to the scene of her husband's murder at midnight? He finished making his decision once I was actually in the passenger seat. He rolled up the other sleeve as we drove the few miles to Billy Roy's last campsite.

"There's a trail of sorts," he said after we parked in a small clearing between some roadside scrub trees. "Keep close to me and don't wander off it." His flashlight lit the way.

"Are there snakes?" I asked.

"No, not at night, but these woods are crawling with poison ivy."

I followed his khaki form up and into the woods. Except for Harmon's dim light ahead, everything around us was dark. It was only when I looked up that I could make out any shapes. Trees whose branches stood out against the lighter sky.

We didn't talk. The trail was just a path of beaten down brush and the flat rocks that bred in the hills of eastern Oklahoma were our only firm toeholds as we crept upward. It wasn't easy going, but Harmon was in good shape and I had often accompanied Billy Roy on his hunting trips, so I knew just how to pace myself.

The trail began to angle to the left and it wasn't as steep. Then we came to a clearing. Someone had built a rock-protected fireplace, but we passed the slabs in silence except for the rustle of the first fall leaves on the ground and went on a few hundred yards to the next clearing. It was higher up the mountain and more to the left of the first campsite.

There was another rock fireplace, but the rocks weren't as symmetrical as the first. I recognized it as Billy Roy's favorite campsite. Leaves covered the ground here, too, but seemed more beaten down. They didn't rustle as much as the ones in the earlier clearing.

"The sheriff's men really searched around here today," Harmon explained. "There's nothing here to see, even if you could see, that is." He sounded almost apologetic that I wouldn't get to see any blood stains or brain bits laying about.

That wasn't what I went there for anyway.

"His body was found here." Harmon pointed to a piece of ground illuminated in a circle by his flashlight. "On his back. By another hunter, but you know that."

I wandered out of the circle of light, out of the circle of the campsite—into the woods.

Harmon aimed the light around the campsite in widening revolutions.

"Hey, where'd you go?" There was a rising panic in his voice.

"I'm here." I stepped back into the lighted arch of his flashlight. "I just had to go to the bathroom."

"Oh, well, what else do you want to see?" He seemed more irritated than embarrassed.

I sat down on one of the flat rocks of the campfire and judging from Harmon's grim expression, probably right where Billy Roy's shot head had been found.

"Nothin'. I just wanted to make sure. In my mind. I wanted to see how everything looked. I couldn't go to sleep tonight until I knew how everythin' looked. We can go now." I stood up.

Harmon and I didn't say much of nothing driving back home. This was only the beginning for the two of us and we knew it. But we couldn't say anything yet. It wasn't the right thing to do. We just rattled along the fireroad in silence until we came to the main highway back to town.

Like I said, it wasn't all that far.

The pale green glow of the dash, the bouncing seats, the lateness of the hour, the secrecy of our visit: all were part of the tension that the unusual circumstances produced. There was some sexual feelings riding in that truck with us, too, gliding around us like the tree shapes along the road. The feelings and the trees were actually present, but as you came up on them, you couldn't see them as clear as you could when you were far off.

We exchanged a formal handshake before I got out.

"Thank you for takin' me up there. I know it seems silly, but I had to go."

"It's okay. I hope it helped you."

"Oh, yes. Except I should have listened to you. I'm afraid I did get poison ivy when I went into the woods to go to the bathroom."

"What makes you think that?"

I held my sweater-covered arms out in front of me and pushed up the sleeves. "My arms itch."

"That's foolish, Bonita Faye. No one gets poison ivy that quickly. It takes several hours before it starts swelling. Your sweater is probably just scratchy." He walked me up the porch. We stood in front of the brightly lit oval glass door.

I slid the sleeves of the sweater back over my arms.

"Yes, of course, you're right. Harmon, are you going to tell anyone . . . Sheriff Hoyle . . . or anyone about takin' me up there tonight?"

"Nah, it was personal, wasn't it? Isn't it?" The question hung like an invisible line between us.

"Yes, of course. Whatever you think is best." I ducked my head to break the thread holding us and went inside. Before I shut the door, before Harmon turned and walked away, I added, "Thank you, Harmon. It meant more to me than you'll ever know for you to help me."

THREE

My mama had named me Bonita Faye. It means "pretty Faye" in Spanish. I wished she had gone all the way and called me "Belle" and dropped the Faye part. I like French better than Spanish. Anything French.

When I wore my real Paris nightgown and strutted around our bedroom, Billy Roy used to roll around on the bed where he was watching me and just laugh. Then he'd say in a voice that wasn't laughing, "Come here, Frenchy. Let me show you what us G.I.s do to little French girls."

Only he wasn't ever no G.I. I never did know what he did during the war. Same as he did after, I guess. Not much of nothing. Some moonshining. Guiding hunting or fishing groups of city men. Knocking around on automobiles. . . . making those pre-war rattletraps accelerate into a post-war world.

He was finishing a fishing trip for some Hot Springs visitors when I met up with him. They had packed their gear and driven away to take their mineral baths at the spas and Billy Roy had gone to clear out the signs of the campsite. Billy Roy weren't that clean minded, but he wanted to make sure it was safe to come back there again for the good fishing. It was private property and Billy Roy didn't hold the deed, but the fishermen never knew it.

So, he was kicking down the rocks that had surrounded the campfire and covering it with leaves and sticks when I crossed through the clearing he had made for his customers. It was illegal for me to be there, too, but, like Billy Roy, I knew there was good fishing in the deep water by the creek. Mama and I were hungry and the fish I caught would be the only meal we said grace over that day.

"Hey, you. What in the hell do you think you're doing here?" he'd yelled at me. "This here's private property." That's just like Billy Roy, attacking when he should of been running himself.

He was half-crouched on the ground and he threw himself out in a wide lunge to grab my ankle as I ran by. He wasn't gentle and he scuffled awful hard to get me to be still. During his tussling he found out I weren't no boy, though I didn't have much girl parts to show around. His hands were rough and he felt around my body like he had a right to. Holding me down with his arm across my throat, he made sure there were no boy parts hid in my overalls.

He surprised me then. After taking some liberal dips into my anatomy, he just pulled his hand free and slapped me on my bottom.

I was pretty good at getting away from freehanded men, but Billy Roy had caught me unawares, so he had the advantage. I knew when I was caught good and was prepared to lose this one. Not expecting no leniency and getting it was what kept me from scrambling up and away from there. He couldn't of caught me when I was prepared.

"Who are you, girl?"

"Who the hell are you?" I asked right back. I sat hunkered on my legs ready to run.

Billy Roy weren't no Robert Taylor, but he had enough of the dark good looks that were famous in the movies to get by on. I took in his worn, dirty corduroys and buttonless flapping sleeves. A stained felt hat was worn low down on his forehead, almost to his eyes. His black eyes were the prettiest thing about him. And sometimes the ugliest. It never did matter what all he said with his mouth, it was always the words in his eyes that I came to listen to.

When he caught me that day in the clearing, they were laughing eyes. And tired. It ain't easy catering to high-falutin' rich city men. He'd just spent twenty-four hours busting his ass making sure every one of them sons-of-the-city had caught a big fish to carry home on their stringers nestled down by a straw-covered block of fast-melting ice in the trunk of their big automobile. Now it was over and he had a little cash in his pocket, and the promise of more the next time they come.

Billy Roy was feeling good, not mean like he was most of the time. And I had to go and meet him when he weren't like himself. It was like my being named Bonita instead of Belle. It was a good idea, it just wasn't quite on the mark.

We weren't much good in geography, so we didn't ever know if we met in Arkansas or Oklahoma. I always meant to go back and find out for sure, but when I knew enough to know how to tell, I didn't care enough to know after all.

Mama died when she met Billy Roy. Oh, not on the first "Howdy-do," but not long after. She said he was weasely and crafty enough to take care of me, not that most of it would be any good, but I'd get by. And then she just up and died.

We lived hand-to-mouth in Mama's house. She and I had wasn't, we said it was ours. Now it was Billy Roy's and mine.

We had some fun. I learned to drink whiskey. And to like doing sex. And to hide from Billy Roy when his eyes were mean.

One of his regular clients was from Mena not far from where we lived. He was a banker and was always bringing rich clients out to hunt and fish and drink so as to get them to do business with his bank.

One day, sometime in forty-eight, his big car broke down in our yard. He'd been out to arrange for Billy Roy to take another group of fellas to our special fishing hole. The one where Billy Roy and I met. It might of been private property, but no one ever showed up to claim it, so we kept on fishing it. Billy Roy said the owner probably died in the war. We felt like it was our place and would even go up there by ourselves to fish and do loving by a campfire.

Anyway, when the banker's car broke down, Billy Roy just laughed and said, "Never you no mind, Judge, I'll fix it up with a bang and a toot." Billy Roy called our benefactor "Judge" 'cause he said calling him "Banker" didn't sound right. I guess it was all right though, 'cause the man never corrected him.

Now when Billy Roy banged and tooted on the car so that it ran better than it had before, the Judge was impressed. It wasn't long after that when he offered to set Billy Roy up in the automotive business. His bank had foreclosed on a service station on the highway into Mena and the Judge wanted Billy Roy to make a go of it. He made him a good deal on the profits and said we could live in the house behind the station's office.

So that's how we moved to town.

But I made Billy Roy marry me first. And that's when he got me the Paris nightgown. He bought it from a real G.I. down on his luck. The soldier had really been in Paris, France, when he bought it and had carried it with him for years, looking for a ladylove to put inside it. He never found one and now, he needed cash more. Or it might of been whiskey Billy Roy traded for it. I forget.

Maybe it was just a little ole gas station, but it was the first for sure place I had a legal right to live in. So I started in fixing it up like it was a real home. I didn't know no grand things to do, but I knew cleanliness helped. My mama had done some cleaning for folks in her time and she always said she didn't know if rich folks were clean or if clean folks were rich.

My first step was to start washing up everything in sight. Billy Roy said nobody noticed if my cabinets were clean inside when the doors were closed, but I got a great satisfaction from knowing that behind them closed doors were four matching drinking glasses, sparkling on clean white butcher paper next to six unchipped blue chiny plates. Next I saved up and bought Fiestaware a piece at a time. I love colorful things around me.

Billy Roy didn't care that I served potatoes in a bowl on the table instead of from the pot, but he did seem a little impressed the night he noticed two sheets on the bed. Only, of course, he put me down when he did. "Bonita Faye Burnett! What is this? A sheet on the bottom for my ass and another one on top for my tally-wacker? Now, that's class, girl. Let's see if I can make this top sheet stand up all by itself. Well, looky there, I did it." Then he threw off the sheet and said, "Come here, my 'Pretty' Faye, you're all the sheet I need covering me."

That was one of the good times.

Billy Roy spent his days under cars getting grimy and greasy and I spent mine washing away the grime and grease. Whatever he brought in I scrubbed away. Even the greasy stuff he left in me.

We didn't have no babies. And no friends. I had never had one so I didn't miss 'em, and Billy Roy got enough of "friends" when he would shut down the garage part and leave me pumping gas to take the Judge and his buddies off on a hunt.

I loved it when they were gone. I'd get me a grape drink from the cooler, unwrap a Hershey bar and read the magazines I'd bought in the drugstore in Mena. When

a horn would honk I'd go out and fill the tanks and collect the money. When I was alone I'd go back to my stories. I didn't just buy movie-star books either, I picked out anything that had something about France in it, whether it was a complicated news story or a Paris fashion show. I preferred the ones where they told about how post-war Paris was the place to be. That tourists were flocking by the thousands to enjoy strolling down the Champs-Elysees, nodding howdy to each other in French. The pictures, especially in *LIFE*, showed Americans sitting at outside cafes drinking wine with Frenchmen wearing berets while white-aproned waiters hovered over their shoulders to see if their glasses were full.

I'd never drunk any wine, but I knew how it would taste. Like my Grapette, only more so. Someday I knew I was going to walk down that street I couldn't pronounce. I wasn't ready yet, but when I was, I'd go there and I'd get in a taxi, and say, "Take me to the Champs-Elysees." And the driver would say, "*Oui, Madame,*" and that's where we'd go.

FOUR

Doctor Bushy wasn't going to let me go to Billy
Roy's funeral on Thursday, but I said, "Of
course, I'm going. What kind of a wife do you
think I am? People aren't going to care about what I look
like. Especially since they already know everything I got
in my house and what color my underwear is under my
dress. A little calamine lotion ain't going to make any difference to what they think about me now."

"I don't mean that, Bonita Faye. Not how you look. Although it's a sad sight. It's not good for you to have to get
dressed and go out. This is unusually warm September
weather and you'll get to itching terrible and probably
vomit again." Doctor Bushy had come to my house three
times since Patsy called him. He gave me a shot while
he talked to me in the dim light of my bedroom. "This
shot will help the itching, but only if you stay still and
cool."

"I don't want something to help the itching. I want
something to stop it," I said. "And I'm going to Billy Roy's
funeral."

"All right, all right, but only to the church. You're not

going to the cemetery. You might get complications. I swear, Bonita Faye, you got the worse case of poison ivy I ever had to treat. You'd think you wallered in it." Doctor Bushy put the needle away in his black bag and Patsy moved into view from where she'd been watching.

I think it was Patsy. My eyes were swollen shut, but occasionally, I would make the effort to open them and through the slit of light, I could make out who was near me. I didn't like not knowing who was in the room with me.

He left the room and Patsy helped me to dress. Because of the poison ivy and where all it was located, I didn't need to worry about if anyone knew the color of my underwear. I didn't have any on. The dress was a lightweight maternity dress that Patsy had worn with her last pregnancy. She'd dyed it black and sewed a white lace collar from my yellow two-piece onto the neck. I could imagine how I looked in it, but since I couldn't see it, what did it matter anyway?

Patsy had helped me to wash my hair earlier, but there were so many bumps on my head that we couldn't get a comb through it enough to make it look like anything. We got tickled trying to squeeze my swollen feet into a pair of her black shoes.

"Lord, I always wanted small feet like yours and now here you go and grow ones bigger than mine." Patsy was holding onto me under my armpits, about the only place I wasn't covered with rash and calamine. I struggled to stand up and she struggled to hold me there.

"We shouldn't be laughing so, Bonita Faye. Not considering where we're fixing to go." But we just laughed harder. I know now it's called "gallows humor"—hysterical laughter about something that's deadly serious and not at all funny.

We settled down proper enough though when Mr. Wilson's black limousine pulled up in front. There's something about that black car of death rolling up to your door that makes a believer out of all skeptics. Patsy took me under one armpit and her husband Jerry took the other and we made it to the funeral car and to the church.

If there hadn't of been a murder involved, probably nobody much would have come to Billy Roy's funeral. But since he died like he did, you'd athought they were burying the mayor. It was that crowded. Even the "Judge" was there.

I didn't see any of it. What I could have seen was blocked by the black veil Patsy had clapped on my head before we went out the front door. Sometimes when I strained my eyes open—through a tear in the net—I could see some candles flickering and a shiny reflection on Billy Roy's gray coffin.

Once Billy Roy turned his truck around on the highway and went back and hit a dog the second time 'cause he didn't kill it the first time. I was with him and I still remember the look in the crippled dog's eyes when the truck bore down on him the second time. I remember that and the splat.

"Well, we buried him good, didn't we, Bonita Faye?" asked Miss Dorothy.

When I didn't answer, she went on while following me and Patsy and Jerry down the church steps. "He was a good man, Bonita Faye. Whatever are you going to do without him?"

I turned around and vomited through the veil on Miss Dorothy's feet.

It had taken 'til Thursday to bury Billy Roy 'cause it was murder. Doctor Bushy was also the coroner and he was a well respected man. So, instead of sending Billy Roy to Tulsa, they let Dr. Bushy do the autopsy right there at Mr. Wilson's.

Harmon told me over the telephone—I wouldn't let him come see me while I had the poison ivy—that the autopsy wasn't no big deal. Doctor Bushy just pulled shotgun pellets out of Billy Roy's head and said he was "killed by a shotgun blast to the face . . . right in the eyes."

And they thought it was Billy Roy's own shotgun 'cause

they couldn't find it no matter how the sheriff's men and volunteers beat down the brush on the mountain.

I didn't much care. Billy Roy was dead and I hurt something awful with all that poison in my system.

I lay in bed. September had turned cold like it always does sooner or later and I alternated from freezing without any covers on my body to breaking out in a sweat from trying to keep warm in a blanket that held in the heat of the poisoned parts of my body.

When I developed pneumonia, Doctor Bushy wanted to send me to the hospital in Fort Smith, but I was too sick to move.

Patsy watched over me night and day. The church ladies didn't come. Guess all they knew to do was clean. 'Sides, Patsy told me they were that upset when Harmon Adams told Sheriff Hoyle about our midnight trip up Cavanal Hill.

"I had to, Bonita Faye. Hoyle wanted to know how you got the poison ivy. I won't tell you what all he was suspecting, but now it's all settled. Boy, did he chew my ass out for taking you up there. At night. And without him. This case is in his official jurisdiction, you know. He told me I shoulda called him immediately, before we went up there. Just as soon as you called me."

Harmon explained all this again to me when he came to see me. I finally let him before October was over. When the swelling went down and the coughing was better.

It was Harmon, and Patsy, of course, that kept me going those weeks. I would lie in bed rubbing one foot against the other 'cause I didn't dare scratch anywhere and the tops and bottoms of my feet were the only places where I didn't have any active poison spots. Also, I allowed myself to scratch one little spot on my elbow. Heaven can't be as sweet as the relief of being able to scratch someplace that itches.

Patsy had the telephone company put in a long cord so I could talk to Harmon while I was in bed. His calls were a lifeline.

After all the sickness, I only weighed about eighty pounds. I don't know how Harmon could stand to look at me. But he always allowed that I looked beautiful to him. He'd sit by my bed and talk to me and listen while I blabbered to him.

And he didn't laugh once when I told him about Paris, France.

The scandal of my being up on the mountain at midnight with Harmon Adams the night after my husband was killed died down. Doctor Bushy finally let me get up and get around. It was too cold to sit on the porch swing, so I sat most of the time wrapped up in a comforter in the living room, looking out the window or reading my books.

The church ladies forgave me and there was always good food . . . to tempt my appetite . . . in the oven or in the refrigerator. I even found out that it was Berta Hoyle who knew how to get rust stains out of the toilet bowl.

By the time Doctor Bushy let Harmon take me for a ride in his pickup, the whole thing was forgotten. Well, almost. There were no leads on Billy Roy's killer, but Sheriff Hoyle said he was "still working on it. I expect the case to break soon."

When it did all I had left of the poison ivy was a small permanent scar on my elbow. And weak eyes. I never did see as good again.

FIVE

Billy Roy and I did all right there in Mena with the gas station and he got a lot of respect for knowing how to fix up cars so they could keep on running. Nobody had any money, not even the rich ones, to buy new cars.

Just like the Depression never touched our neck of the woods—everyone was too poor to know they was poorer—the post-war prosperity was just as ignored. Mena weren't no boom town and never will be. Like most small towns in the Ozarks, people just lived there without any special reason to do so. I don't even know how come I was there.

There was a little more money though. I was saving coins in my second orange Fiestaware iced tea pitcher. Billy Roy broke the first and he wasn't even drunk. When he found the coins, he said I was stealing from him. And I said, was not, they was tips for when I pumped the gas when he was gone fishing.

We was there about a year when the Judge come up with another idea.

"We foreclosed on another garage, Billy Roy. It's

bigger than this one and there'll be more money in it for you and your 'little bit.' There's a dealership on the side. Yes, sir, I think we can clean up on this one. Of course, you'll have to move. To Oklahoma. But, hey, look at it this way. You're moving up in the world."

I was surprised. I didn't think even anyone from Mena would think moving to Poteau, Oklahoma, was "moving up in the world." Believe me when I tell you that there are no pedigrees in Poteau. You got your Sooners, your Indian "heritage," your transported Arkies and a whol' lot of good ol' boys.

However, I got to admit they weren't doing a half-bad job. Especially those into the second and third generation of hardscrabblers. Nice thing about Billy Roy and me moving there, nobody asked anything about your background, who your folks were and all. They were afraid if they asked you, you'd feel like you had a right to ask them back.

We moved to Poteau in 1950. I was barely twenty-two years old. But, of course, we're only counting years, not aging.

It was a good business. The Burnett Ford Dealership and Service Garage. The only reason the previous owner had failed was 'cause he had gotten over excited with the idea of selling new cars to people who hadn't seen them in five years and had grown too fast. He'd started a dealership in Muskogee, Henryetta, and some other place at the same time. There was only so much money to go around and the busted dealer couldn't get it all.

We even got his house in town. Two blocks off the main highway and four blocks from the railroad track. It was an old house: four rooms and the added bathroom. I liked having an inside toilet. We'd had one in Mena, but had to share it with the gas station customers. I didn't like cleaning up after strangers.

Billy Roy made me use my coins to furnish and fix up the house. "What else on this earth, Bonita Faye, could you be saving it for?"

The first friend he made was Miss Dorothy over at the post office. "Got to do my public relations and that woman knows everyone. She'll spread the word about us. You be nice to her, you hear? And invite her over for your fried chicken."

Miss Dorothy was Billy Roy's age. You'd a thought he was courting her for more than her goodwill the way he carried on about her visit.

It was on Sunday after church. We had been in town six weeks. I fixed my fried chicken, perfect as always. And there wasn't a lump one in my milk gravy or mashed potatoes.

Miss Dorothy had insisted on bringing the dessert and brought what she called her famous pineapple upside-down cake. Billy Roy acted like he had never had none before. If that's public relations selling, Billy Roy sure bought a lot of it that night.

We ate in the kitchen off the Fiestaware. I'd worked up to three full place settings by then. Glad she was "Miss" Dorothy, not "Mrs." or one of us wouldn't of eaten. And I know who that would have been. Billy Roy got the dark blue, Miss Dorothy, the yellow, and I kept the orange dishes for myself.

"That was so fine, Mrs. Burnett," Miss Dorothy said when we'd finished the chicken and I was cutting her squishy cake.

"Call her Bonita Faye, Miss Dorothy," said my husband.

"Well, it'd be an honor . . . Billy Roy." And those two fools burst out laughing like they was sharing a secret joke. "Bonita Faye, dear, you're an excellent little cook. My little ol' cake will just be an embarrassment after that scrumptious meal."

"On the contrary, Miss Dorothy," said Billy Roy. On the contrary! Where did Billy Roy ever learn to say, "On the contrary"?

"We coulda thrown out Bonita Faye's chicken and just dined on this lovely dessert alone and had enough to satisfy the most hungry man," said my husband. He ate his piece of cake in two forkfuls and jumped up to cut himself another.

What was left of the cake I pushed down his throat in the bedroom that night saying, "On the contrary, my ass, Miss Dorothy," with every bite I shoved in his mouth with the heel of my hand. Billy Roy was choking to death with laughter and Miss Dorothy's cake. He stuck his tongue out and pulled the pineapple ring I had hung over his nose into his mouth. It left slimy golden goo over his face. Still choking and laughing, he said, "Now, Belle baby, that's public relations. Just see if it don't pay off."

I had to wash my Paris nightgown out real careful to get all that pineapple gunk off it. And I still thought I could see a stain on the hem.

He was right though. Miss Dorothy talked to everyone in town at least once a day through her switchboard and she went on and on about "that nice Mr. Burnett and his sweet, young wife. He's the one who is the new Ford dealer. Knows everything there is to know about cars."

Joining the Lions Club helped with public relations, too. Billy Roy and me drove to Fort Smith and bought him a suit and he joined those fellas every Tuesday noon for lunch at the local cafe. They'd put up their little blue banner in the corner and act like they was in a private dining room. And they all talked about the future of Poteau. What killed me, they asked Billy Roy's opinion on "which direction the town should take now?" Like he knew!

The Thursday night card game—with free booze—in back of the dealership didn't hurt Billy Roy's civic standing either. Or him finding the best fishing holes and taking one or two of them with him when they came to calling about buying a new car. And hunting—why, there wasn't a creature that flew, swam, crawled or walked on four feet that didn't come running when Billy Roy Burnett cocked his gun or dropped his line.

Big money changed hands at the card games, and Billy

Roy, as lucky with cards as with striped bass, let many a debt go uncollected. "Look at it this way, Bonita Faye, I didn't have the money in the first place so I don't exactly lose anything. And I gained something—they're in debt to me. It's pure public relations."

"What if you lose, Billy Roy?"

"Not with my cards, Belle baby, not with my cards."

SIX

"We know who killed your husband, Bonita Faye," said Sheriff Hoyle almost two months to the day after Billy Roy died.

"Who?" I asked. That one word was all I could manage. My hand shook as I poured hot coffee in my orange Fiestaware cup. Sheriff Hoyle was holding the yellow one in his beefy hands, his elbows on my kitchen table.

"His name was Steuben Ross from near Winslow." Sheriff Hoyle slid his eyes over to me in triumph like he had just handed me the winning ticket on the daily double at Oaklawn.

"Was?"

"Yep, he's dead, too. Died two days after Billy Roy." The coffee was really hot and the sheriff's eyes, the only thing I could focus on, stared out at me over the rising steam.

"So."

Disappointed in my reaction, Sheriff Hoyle became more talkative. And sheriff-like. He gave me the details like he had probably written them in his report.

"Steuben Ross, 28, of Washington County, Arkansas,

was killed when his pickup went over the side of Mt. Gaylor the Monday after Billy Roy was murdered. Although the state patrol got his body out of the wreck, they couldn't do nothing about the truck. Finally, though, a wrecker from Mountainburg pulled it up. He . . . the wrecker . . . is used to getting cars and trucks off the side of the mountain. Pulled it up last"—Sheriff Hoyle referred to his brown Aladdin notebook—"last Thursday morning."

"But how do they know he killed Billy Roy?"

Sheriff Hoyle handed me the information like this time he was giving me the winning ticket in the feature race. "They found Billy Roy's rifle in the bed of the truck."

"That don't mean he did it."

"Well, Bonita Faye, it's called circumstantial evidence." When Sheriff Hoyle spoke legal words, he did it slow and deliberately. He peeked at his notes. "Ross, a convicted 'shiner from around Winslow, was reported camping on Cavanal Hill the Saturday night Billy Roy was killed." The sheriff looked up at me. "There was two people who have identified his truck as being the one that was reported being at the scene of the crime. You know, at the base of the mountain . . . on the side of the road?"

He went on. "They're hunters from Fort Smith. The officer in charge drove them up to the wrecker's garage in Mountainburg yesterday and showed them the truck. They identified it because of its unusual color." He stammered for the right description. "You know . . . bile green."

"Chartreuse."

"What?"

"Chartreuse," I said. "That's what that kind of green color is called. It's French, I think."

"Bonita Faye, I don't know no French, but I do know that we got two men who say that same truck was on the side of the road the night Billy Roy was killed. Where

Billy Roy was killed. And Billy Roy's rifle was in his truck bed. That's circumstantial evidence and we say Steuben Ross killed Billy Roy and threw the rifle in the back of the truck and lit out for Winslow." He put his little notebook on top of his coffee cup and although the coffee had cool'd some, little wisps of steam came up either side of the wide cup and curled the notepaper with the moisture.

"Now what do you say?" he asked.

"Did he have a family . . . this Steuben man, I mean?"

"Nah, well, yes. Sorta. His wife died giving birth to their little girl four years ago. She was being raised by her grandma, but the old lady died late in August. That's why the little girl was with Ross when he shot Billy Roy."

"What, he killed Billy Roy when he had his kid with him? How do you know that, Sheriff?" For the first time I started getting hysterical.

Pleased at my response, Sheriff Hoyle picked up his damp notebook and pressed the pages straight before the flipped them to the one he wanted. "Says so right here. Four-year-old girl . . . named Ellen . . . or Elly, as they call her . . . remembers going camping with her papa right afore he died in the truck."

"How can a child that small remember something like that?"

"Oh, she remembers all right. Although some of it is baby talk. Like the bells."

"Bells, what about bells?"

"This girl . . . this Elly . . . was living with her papa then, after the grandma died. He went hunting clear to Poteau . . . but most probably delivering 'shine 'cause he didn't have his own rifle with him in the truck." Sheriff Hoyle paused to read the next page. "They got there late at night and he drug the little girl . . . this Elly . . . up the mountain in the dark. Sat her down on some stones around a campfire . . . only he didn't light no fire." Sheriff Hoyle was now reading direct from his notes. I was amazed at how well he had written them down from whoever he got them from.

"Ross left the child alone while he went back to the truck." The sheriff looked up at me. "Now ain't that a shameful thing for a daddy to do? Leaving his baby alone on a mountaintop in the middle of the night?" He went back to the notes. "Elly heard church bells and gun shots going off at the same time. She was scared, but before she could start crying, her papa was standing beside her. Scared her, him coming up so quiet like. He grabbed her up and half fell down the mountain with her to the truck. They got in the truck and went home. Drove all night. She says she slept and when she woke up, she was in her papa's cabin. There, Miss Bonita Faye. There's your circumstantial evidence."

I said, "There ain't any church on that mountain."

He sighed and said, "I know. We figure she heard some kind of clanging. Mighta sounded like bells to her."

"Where is she now?"

"Who?"

"That baby, that Elly. Where is she now?" I needed to know.

"Life is funny, Bonita Faye. That little girl is sitting in the catbird seat now."

"What do you mean?"

"After they pulled Ross out of the truck—she wasn't in the accident—they turned her over to welfare. Put her in a foster home, but she only stayed three days. A family from Fayetteville, a professor and his wife adopted her. The man's a big muckety-muck from the university and they already got everything legal. When the local sheriff's men interviewed her, they said she was sitting in a big playroom dressed up in a pink dotted swiss dress with a satin bow in her hair clutching a doll as big as she is."

I refilled the sheriff's cup. My hands weren't shaking no more.

Sheriff Hoyle sipped the scalding liquid. "Ain't life funny, Bonita Faye?"

I poured my own cup. "How so, Sheriff?"

"That little girl has gone from a shiner's shack in the mountains to a storybook home in town. And, you." He took a bigger sip. "You lost a husband, but you got all that insurance money." He put down his cup. "Whatcha gonna do with all that money, Bonita Faye?"

It was cooler in Paris in the springtime than I thought it would be.

SEVEN

I didn't ever hear another word about Elly Ross, the little girl who was up on the mountain with her father when Billy Roy was killed.

That's a lie.

If I'm going to tell this right, tell it like it really happened, then I've got to say the lie.

I knew every new dress that little girl had. Compliments of Mary Abbott, saleswoman at Sook's Tot and Teen Exclusive Togs of Fayetteville and Patsy's cousin. And I knew the results of every report card she ever received from Fayetteville Westside Elementary, Washington Irving Junior High, and Fayetteville High schools. Compliments of Homer Shipman, assistant school superintendent and Mary's son-in-law.

Through them I knew when red was Elly's favorite color and when she switched to blue. Whether she and her mom were buying satin bows for her blond pigtails or headbands for a bob.

I sighed over Elly's math grades. I understood the problem. But from multiplication tables to high school

geometry she hung in there and passed through her
school years with grades on the plus side.

Oh, it cost me a pretty penny for all that confidential
information. But I had the insurance money at first, and
then the income from my business venture. It was worth
it to me to know exactly when Elly was going to summer
horse camp in Siloam Springs and when she was first fit-
ted for braces by the local orthodontist.

I have all her school pictures. Sometimes I would just
line them up in a row, all those little 2 by 1½ color pho-
tos and marvel at the miracle of her unfolding. I spent
hours squinting at those colorful little pieces, trying to
see beyond the photographic paper, trying to see if Elly
was happy, trying to recognize a real person inside the
pictures, trying to see if she had a soul.

There were insignificant gaps, but I knew most everything I needed to know about the kind of life she led with
her adopted parents. How spoiled she was, but sweet
and appreciative. She was a good and loving daughter to
the professor and his wife, the only child they ever had.

She was about seventeen when I met her in person.
Almost seventeen. Two months and three days before
she became seventeen.

I was invited to an administrative's wives tea at the
university. Harmon was lecturing to the University Law
School on Criminology and the Law at a big legal seminar and the spouses who attended were entertained by
the wife of the university's president. I suggested it.
Thought it would be nice if some of the professors' wives
and their families socialized with the seminar's partici-
pants. Wasn't like they hadn't done it before.

And I helped make out the guest list, seeing as how I
was the liaison between the seminar lecturers and the
school.

"I'll bet you're a cheerleader," I said to Elly. The first
words I ever said to her felt dumb and inadequate.

"How did you know?" she asked. Lord, she looked
beautiful. Her hair was shiny and fluffed out like a movie

star's. She was tall and graceful and athletic and stylish looking. Her blue eyes were clear and intelligent. She had on a turquoise cotton shirtwaist dress that I didn't know she had. Since she had passed on from the Tots and Teens shop, I didn't know where she bought her clothes. I'd have to find out.

"Oh, it was a wild guess," I said. "What else are you interested in?"

Like I didn't know.

"Reading, tennis."

How's that for well-rounded?

"But mostly music, the theatre." Elly was answering me, holding a cut glass cup full of pink punch, but there was a slight introspective quality about her answer. Like she was making a list for herself as well as for me.

"Any special kind of music?"

"Mozart. I play the piano." Didn't I know that? Didn't I have tapes of her practicing and playing? And years of recitals?

"I like Mozart, too," I said. "I have a tape of some music played on his own pianoforte by a famous Austrian musician. I bought it at Mozart's house, well, it's really a museum now in Salzburg. I'll send it to you if you like."

"Do you? Would you?" Elly really looked at me for the first time. I wasn't just another face in the university's parlor any longer. As I became more real, her eyes narrowed and for the first time, focused on me, Bonita Faye Adams. The years had been kind to me. I'd softened and rounded a bit. Not as much as now, but it was a flattering effect. About that time I was probably the prettiest I ever would be.

"You've been to Salzburg?" she asked.

"Oh, yes. You ought to go. Especially for the Festival. It's beautiful. The city's so old and the streets are so narrow. At Festival time, there's music everywhere and flowers. Ten thousand tulips alone in the garden of the main public building. But the music is king during Festival." I stopped and looked directly at Elly. I didn't want to bore her or worse, have her thinking I was putting on airs. I had added Salzburg to my last year's summer European itinerary only when I found out Mozart was her favorite composer. I'd loved it, too. All I had ever known of Salzburg before my trip was that was where they had filmed *The Sound of Music*. Now I'd been to Mozart's home and my appreciation of his wonderful music I owed to this teenager.

"Where are you from again?" she asked. Elly became interested in me and bent her head forward. The movement framed us together and set us apart from the others. I relished the intimacy.

"Oklahoma City. My husband's the new head of the Oklahoma State Bureau of Investigation. He's one of the lecturers at the seminar." If I didn't have my own respectable credentials, I wasn't above using Harmon's.

"And you've been to Austria? To Europe?"

That was credentials enough for my Elly.

"Did you go in a group or just you and your husband?" Something in my eyes must have communicated to her because she half-started and exclaimed in an excited voice. "Oh, I know. You went by yourself. I want to do that, too."

"Well, almost by myself. I have an adopted French son about your age. I accompany him back to Paris every year and then, yes, I do travel on through Europe on my own. And sometimes with friends."

Elly reached out and grabbed the elbow of a passing woman. "Mommy, I want you to meet my new friend, Mrs. Adams. And, Mommy, guess what? Mrs. Adams has been to Europe and she knows Mozart."

"Not personally, I hope," said the small well groomed woman with the laughing gray eyes.

And that was my introduction to Elly, the only daughter I'll ever have. You can see what I did later, I did 'cause I owed her.

EIGHT

Patsy always knew that I had killed Billy Roy Burnett up on Cavanal Hill.

Oh, she never said, "Bonita Faye, I know you killed Billy Roy up on Cavanal Hill," or anything like that.

Just like she never said, "Bonita Faye, I know you climbed that mountain road at night to confront Billy Roy about trying to make you sleep with the Judge and you got mad when he laughed at you, and you took his new shotgun and blew the laughter out of his eyes."

Patsy never challenged me with, "I know you had a double dose of poison ivy 'cause you got the first case scrambling up that trail in the dark, grabbing every foothold and clinging to every vine you could to keep from falling down. You made Harmon take you back up there that night 'cause you knew when you started itching that Sunday afternoon, somebody was going to put two and two together and figure out that you had been up there with Billy Roy."

Patsy didn't go on about the life insurance money. Not even when she could of. She could of said, "Bonita

Faye, what about Billy Roy bragging to you about a month before he died about how he had screwed that obnoxious insurance fellow out of a big policy on himself in exchange for a gambling debt? And while that wasn't foremost on your mind when you left the house after dark on Saturday night . . . it was floating around there in that head of yours . . . floating right up there with the anger you felt when you started to add seventy-two cents to your orange Fiestaware pitcher for your trip to Paris. And you found the money you had saved was gone. Every penny. It was mostly pennies in there anyway, but they had added up so that you were only forty-two dollars short of a one-way ticket to France.

"Forty-two dollars short of getting away from Poteau. Just forty-two dollars short of getting shut of Billy Roy and the meanness in him that had grown as he started to get cocky about his success of being the biggest con man that ever set foot in LeFlore County, Oklahoma.

"And, Bonita Faye, you were the only one Billy Roy trusted to show how he really was. You watched day by day, week by week, month by month as his real self was exposed.

"It was just like watching a rose unfold its petals in the sun on a hot afternoon in June. Where you thought there would be beauty in the unveiling, you were surprised by the corrupt deformity that curled the fresh petals, first at the edges and then throughout the veined perfection of the bloom.

"Where there should have been the fragrance of sweet perfume, there was the putrid odor of dormant corruption released from its lethargic condition by a set of bizarre circumstances.

"A black rose that never should have blossomed."

Patsy never said those words because, bless her heart, she didn't have them in her word-stock. And I didn't either . . . then.

If she had spoken at all of Billy Roy's murder she would have said, "Bonita Faye, honey, I don't blame you one little bit for blowing Billy Roy away. After all, wasn't he coming home every night, sitting at the kitchen table, holding you tight by one wrist to keep you in place and telling you about all the nasty things he had done all day?

"Like hanging around Miss Dorothy's red-brick office building after lunchtimes 'til the poor woman finally shut down the switchboard and closed the post office to give your husband a hot, wet screw on the mildewed Army cot in her back room? And didn't he tell you that night and every night, how it was? The sweat. Her wanting it so bad. How excited she got, slippery even, when Sheriff Hoyle beat on the locked door to see if Miss Dorothy was all right in there.

"How she came then with him holding his hand over her mouth to keep her from screaming with the joy of it. How she bit and then sucked those dirty, oil-stained fingers. How with sweat and mascara running down her face, she had unlocked the door and peered around it to tell the sheriff that she was okay. Just taking a little nap in the back room and that she'd be back on duty as soon as she got woke up good.

"And then Billy Roy would get all excited himself telling you about it. He would twist your wrist tighter and pull you up on your kitchen table, the very same one where you and Harmon ate the chicken, and he would stand at the end of it and push himself into you, his head arched back, his eyes closed and a thin smile on his lips. And when he finally pulled away with a wet sucking sound, he'd tell you that you wasn't as good as Miss Dorothy.

"But that you were probably good enough for the Judge. 'The Judge has been making noises about you, Bonita Faye.' Only Billy Roy called you 'Belle, baby,' like he always done.

"You lay on the table with your legs still up and your

dress clean up to your boobs and your apron still over your eyes and he told you what he had set up for the Judge and you. That the Judge had gone wild when Billy Roy had told him about your real Paris nightgown and you was to wear it when Billy Roy took you to the Judge's cabin next month. Everyone was supposed to think it was another fishing trip. The Judge was going to give you twenty-five dollars for your orange Fiestaware pitcher. 'Just think on that, Belle, baby.'

"Bonita Faye, I know that when you didn't go to that fishing lodge with the Judge that Billy Roy took your one-way ticket to France money and bought himself a new shotgun. And that you realized that when you was putting your seventy-two cents in the pitcher after he'd gone hunting for the weekend.

"I understand the red haze that exploded in your head. I understand the way you arched your own back, threw back your own head and smiled your own thin little smile.

"You tore out of that kitchen. Out of that house. It was dark by then. Way past sunset. You headed for that mountaintop and Billy Roy Burnett.

"There were no cars on the road as you stalked up that road. You walked fast; almost ran. You weren't even sweating none when you come to the base of the mountain. Only a slight sheen of moisture all over your body, but mostly on your upper lip. Your breathing was easy. Only a gutteral-like snort ever dozen breaths or so even gave lie to how the pace had got to you. Like a horse after a race.

"You sure surprised Billy Roy some when you walked into the light of his campfire. He was right prideful of how he was a natural woodsman and he hadn't heard you coming atall. He was sprawled on the ground, his head on one of the rocks that he had pulled away from those that circled the fire. A bottle of booze was in his hands, almost cradled in his arms. He'd lifted the bottle to take a drink when you burst into the light. He dropped the bottle and it hit the rock, splattering glass and booze all around. Enough to make the fire sizzle and burn blue for a second.

"Billy Roy grabbed his shotgun. The new one you had bought him without your knowing. He'd leveled it at you afore he recognized it was his own wife he was aiming at. When he did know it was you, he'd been mad . . . mean mad. He started yelling at you.

"And you'd yelled back. You never had before and this confused him. There was all fire shadows of moving bodies and leafy tree limbs. And you said right out, but in a low voice, 'Billy Roy Burnett, did you take my one-way-ticket-to-France money out of my orange Fiestaware pitcher and buy yourself that shotgun?'

"Billy Roy just doubled up and laughed. Laughed so hard, he dropped the shotgun. Laughed so hard all you could hear was him snorting out loud and choking. 'Belle, Belle, Belle.' Then lower, he'd snickered, 'Is that what that money was for? Is that what you been saving your pennies for? To go to France? To Paris, fuckin' France?'

"You said, yes, you was going to France. That you was going to get away from him. That he had changed or maybe he was now what he'd always meant to be. Mean and bad and nasty. Your mama had been right when she'd said you'd have some bad times with Billy Roy Burnett and she'd been wrong, too. You wouldn't 'get by' with Billy Roy. You hissed at him, spluttering spit through your teeth while you told him you was going to France to get away from him. You was going to go where people were gentle, refined and said 's 'il vous plait' instead of 'gimme' and 'merci' instead of 'fuck you' and 'ooh-la-la' instead of 'bullshit.'

"Billy Roy quit laughing and grabbed both your wrists and shook you till your teeth rattled and your eyes ached in your head. Then he twisted you around with one hand and hit you across the shoulders hard with the other. Not on your face where bruises would show. And he thrown you down on the rocks around the fire.

"He said, 'Now listen here to me, Belle, baby, you ain't going nowhere. Ever. You are gonna stay right here with me. And you are going to do what I say . . . and only what I say from now on. I'm tired of being nice to you. You and your high and mighty airs. I swear, Belle, baby, I don't know where you get your fancy ideas, you ain't ever been nothing but dirt yourself. You come from dirt and you're going to stay dirt all your life. The next time I set you up with the Judge . . . or any jack-leg that comes down the pike . . . you're going to drop your jeans or raise your skirt and fuck like a bunny. That's all you're good for anyways. Forget about your Paris, France. It's all a big lie anyhow. Real people, Belle, baby, don't ever say no *"ooh-la-la."* '

"They was still sparks swirling from the fire where your tumble had shifted the burning logs. You noticed them as your head cleared enough so your eyes could focus. The firm hardness under your body was not just rocks. You had fallen on Billy Roy's shotgun.

"Bonita Faye, I know what happened next. As you reached under your body your finger found the trigger on that shotgun. Billy Roy was looking in his pack for another bottle of booze when you said quietlike, 'Maybe they don't say no *"ooh-la-la,"* Billy Roy. But I do know one thing they really say.'

"Like always when Billy Roy had spent his temper, he was in a good mood. He found his bottle, clutched it by the neck and turned to share a swig with you. As long as you were here he'd have some fun with you. His eyes were laughing when he asked, 'What's that, Belle, baby? What do they really say?'

"Bonita Faye, you leveled that new shotgun right at his eyes and said, 'They really say *au revoir* for goodbye.'

"Then you pulled the trigger."

Now my friend Patsy didn't say any of that. She didn't

even know to say how it all happened. But Patsy always knew that I had killed Billy Roy Burnett up on Cavanal Hill.

Patsy is the best friend I ever had.

NINE

I worried about Elly's soul . . . searching for signs of it in every school picture 'cause I spent so much time looking in my own bathroom mirror . . . searching for signs of my own.

Now, of course, I know souls don't look back out of eyes and say "hey, you, I'm in here and all's right with the world."

I know that.

But a soul's something that looks out of an eye and lets you know its there. It's a glint of awareness that keeps the blankness out of a stareback. It ain't God though some say it is. It's an awareness that there is a God and an indication of your personal relationship with Him . . . It . . . Her. . . .

Don't go getting worried any that I'm going to go religious on you. What you do with your glint in your eye is between you and your eye and is no business of mine.

Billy Roy's had shown with meanness and Harmon's with goodness. Little Elly had the glint of innocence and mine, the spark of shrewdness.

Not pretty, but it was mine own. And I learned to accept it.

I don't like surprises. Any surprises. But I am always surprised about how serious people take their religion.

When I was growing up, I didn't even know there was any such thing as religion. Mama certainly never told me nothing about it and I wasn't the beneficiary of many people practicing it. And when I was, it was one of them surprises I didn't like.

You coulda knocked me over with a feather when Mama told me that the Swans were going to send me to church camp. We'd only been working for them about a month. School was out and I was looking forward to roaming free, heading out for some of the back country roads and trailing my bare toes through the hot dust of the barely scraped out tire tracks that passed for a motor trail.

I wanted to smell the dust and the heat and to listen to the chirping things in the trees say, "Lord, ain't it hot?" And the one in the tree next to it would answer, "Lord, it shore is." On they would go, complaining about the heat and passing on their wearisome message like a child's game of Round Robin. I could walk a mile down them tree-shaded lanes and their tiresome chirping of the weather would always be announced right behind me and I'd catch the monotonous answer with my next steps.

Pretty soon I'd wander off the road and find a shady spot where water was trickling through and I would sprawl on the ground and watch the little water things dart back and forth at the edge of the pool. If it was deep enough, and I was still enough, sometimes I'd see a big gar circle near the top of the water or a turtle yawn in the heat from atop a half-surfaced log.

Before I went to Paris, France, that was the only way I thought summers should be spent.

Mr. and Mrs. Swan were Baptists. Good Baptists. They paid my way along with their own twelve-year-old daughter, Little Alice, to a Baptist encampment in Glorietta, New Mexico. I finally agreed to go 'cause I thought I was going to Mexico and would see some Mexicans. Was I surprised when I found out New Mexico was in the United States of America and who I saw, was Indians. My ideas of geography was sadly deficient in those days. It's a wonder I ever found Paris, France.

That set of circumstances was how I found out about religion and the store that people set by it.

Instead of picking up a smooth round rock out of the road and popping it into my mouth to savor the heat and pleasing flavor of dirt, I found myself in the backseat of Mr. Swan's Ford with two other girls on my way to Glorietta, New Mexico, U.S.A.

Mr. Swan prayed afore we started the car for our "safe journey" and when we stopped to eat or go to the bathroom at a gas station he'd pray thanks for our "safe arrival." After we had done our business, he'd start the cycle all over again. "Dear Jesus, Our Lord. Please be with us as we cross this vast country. Keep us safe from careless drivers and evil travelers. Help me to protect my dear wife and sweet daughters of the Light during this trip to New Mexico. In Jesus's name. Amen."

I quickly learned the etiquette of praying. You got real still and looked down at the floorboard of the backseat, watching the spider in the bottom corner of Mr. Swan's seat spin its web. We took that spider clear to New Mexico and back.

We drove straight through. No stopping. When it was dark and us three girls were sleeping, stretched out the best we could in the cramped back seat, I'd woke up and saw the back of Mrs. Swan's head at the steering wheel. The Ford's headlights rushed ahead to search the road for careless drivers and evil travelers while Mrs. Swan softly sang *In the Sweet By and By*. Mr. Swan slept, his head leaned against the window on the passenger side. His snoring kept accompaniment to his wife's singing. I watched awhile and then fell back asleep myself. I dreamed I was being carried to a faraway shore in the hands of a pure white angel who looked like a big, feathered dove.

Glorietta, New Mexico, was a big surprise. Not just that it was in the United States, but that it looked just like the Ozark mountains. The trees were different and the mountains had a little sharper edge to them, but for that we could of been sitting down to have church service right near Queen Willimena Lodge in Arkansas. Instead we set on sawed half logs lined up like church pews in the middle of a raw encampment on the lip of a mountain edge in New Mexico. Behind the preacher's place at the front you stared out at a huge valley full of tall trees. Sometimes the preacher talked about Jesus and God and sometimes we sang. And sometimes, someone behind a bush at the very edge of the mountain would read Bible verses that sounded like God Himself was speaking out of nowhere.

After I got over being scared of hearing a voice with no body tell me to "lift up my eyes unto the hills," I became curious as to who was saying those words. I looked forward to that part of the service. (We had them three times a day.) Everytime I was determined to catch someone coming out of the bushes so I'd know who was speaking to me. I got so excited with the voice in the bushes that I spent my whole time at each service with my eyes on them shrubs.

After three days of Arts and Crafts and Bible Study and Sword Drill, one of the older counselors came over to me. "Bonita Faye, you are so smart and so joyful to teach that we counselors have voted to let you help us in our worship service. We don't know of any other child who has been so eager or so attentive at the services. Since you read so well, we want you to read the Scripture behind the bushes at tomorrow's sunrise service."

Well, flip me over and call me a pancake. I was going behind them bushes.

They gave me my Bible verse to study afore we went

to bed. I had it memorized in all of three minutes, but I spent the rest of the night in my bottom bunk practicing in my head just how I would say it.

Early the next morning I met the counselor down by the worship spot and she showed me the mystery of the talking bush. There was a little rock trail down behind the bushes that you took to come up in a clearing in the middle of them. That way no one ever saw who was in the bushes. She led me there, put a finger to her lips and turned back down the trail.

I couldn't see through the shrubbery, but I could hear the faithful coming to worship. There was rustlings of feet and muffled coughing as they took their places on the split logs. The air was clean and cool. Looking backwards from my hidey-hole I could see clear down the mountain. Trees bigger than the camp's main lodge were thousands of feet below me. Row after row of them marched up the mountainside.

The preacher said his piece and the people sang, their voices sailed past me and flew on out in the valley below. I felt like I was going to wet my pants with the beauty of it all. Finally I heard the preacher give me my cue. I said my Scripture in a clear, loud speech just like I'd practiced in my head. My voice fought the wind, but I held steady and did my part.

After I finished, there was silence. Then the preacher said, "Amen." And the people stood and started back toward the camp. I was so thrilled with my performance that I didn't take the little back trail to the camp. Though they scratched my face as I plowed through, I pushed through the bushes and came out among the campers. They was walking by me in a dazed look, tears streamed down the faces of some of them. "How'd I do?" I asked one of the boys I recognized. He looked at me like he didn't see me. Like he was seeing a foreign shore in his eyes. I tugged at his sleeve. "It's all right. That was me. How was I?" He shrugged away my hand and walked on.

I stood still as the people passed. They flowed by me like ants around a mud puddle.

That's when I first knew that people take their religion so to heart. They didn't want to know, like I had, about the mystery of the talking bush. They didn't want to know it was me speaking. They wanted to believe. In my lifetime since, I've experienced other examples of how sincere folks take their religion, but I was never as surprised about it again as I was that morning that I stood in the bushes on a mountaintop in Glorietta, New Mexico, and said in a sweet innocent voice through the leaves, *"And I heard a great voice out of heaven saying, Behold, the tabernacle of God is with men, and he will dwell with them, and they shall be his people, and God himself shall be with them, and be their God.*

"And God shall wipe away all tears from their eyes; and there shall be no more death, neither sorrow, nor crying, neither shall there be any more pain: for the former things are passed away.

"And he that sat upon the throne said, Behold, I make all things new."

There were only two other surprises at Glorietta. No, make that three. One was the warm way I felt when we sat around the campfire at night and sang "Kumbaya." The second was how I felt when I was one of only two campers who made it to the top of a steep hiking trail. Thin and scrawny, all stick arms and legs, I was the last one the young counselor thought would make it all the way. He and the other camper, a boy, and I left the others along the way. Only the three of us arrived at the summit. After slapping us on the back, the counselor took out his knife and let us carve our names on a tree. I like knowing, even to this day, that high in a pine tree in New Mexico, scratched in its trunk, are the words "Bonita Faye Was Here."

We half slid back down the mountain, picking up the

stragglers as we went. Victorious, we reached the bottom and jumped into the cold stream to cool off and to wash the poison ivy from our scratched and exposed skin. When I killed Billy Roy ten years later, I shoulda remembered that was how you got rid of poison ivy.

My last surprise was when we got into the car for the trip home. I had lowered my head to pray for "our safe journey" and saw blood trickling from my shorts, down my leg. I had started my periods. I watched the spider in its thick web in the corner of the floorboard of the back seat of Mr. Swan's Ford. I knew it was going to be a long trip home.

That was my introduction and education into religion. So this is the very last thing I ever have to say about souls. I found mine looking back at me from the bathroom mirror while I was getting over the poison ivy. Whatever it told me while I was up there leaning over the sink, squinting through swollen eyelids, is my affair and right there in that little old add-on bathroom in Poteau, Oklahoma, is where that business stays.

Let's just say I felt squared away with me and myself and my eyeballs about killing Billy Roy.

TEN

I t took me nearly six months after Billy Roy died
to get everything in order. I had to get over the
poison ivy, get my health back, work on my relationship with Harmon and collect the insurance
money.

When that next spring rolled around I was going to be
ready.

I went around the house singing and humming, *"Mona
Lisa, Mona Lisa . . . la . . . dee . . . daa . . . dee . . . da."*
My U.S.A. passport was in the third right drawer of my
bureau right under my real Paris nightgown. Ever so
often when I was cleaning or cooking or packing, I'd
stop right where I was and hug myself and say, *"Ooh la
la*, Bonita Faye, you're going to Paris, France."

Then talk about surprises.

While I was squaring everything away with God and
the insurance company, Harmon was out making himself
a hero. And once he learned how, he went on to make
himself a double hero. It was just like a double-dose of
poison ivy.

Three convicted killers from the McAlester State

Penitentiary escaped and headed across the open
ground toward the tree groves that surround the prison.
One of the three was a full-bloodied Indian and he led
them other two, hillbillies both, clean out of the search
area. Using tricks he shoulda used to make himself a
credit to his tribe, John Falling Eagle outsmarted the
search parties and their howling hound dogs ever which
way for Christmas. Falling Eagle drug those other losers
through thickets, creeks, and dusty, fallow fields and,
wouldn't you know it, straight into the arms of Oklahoma's finest Highway Patrolman—Harmon Adams.

All I knew of what was going on was from the radio.
I didn't see or hear from Harmon the four days the fugi-
tives were on the loose. Well, one phone call to say,
"Bonita Faye, you stay inside your house and lock the
doors. Better yet, go stay with Patsy, but if you do stay
home, get Billy Roy's shotgun from the closet, load it and
keep it with you at all times . . . even in the bathroom. I
got to go now. I love you, Bonita Faye."

There . . . he'd said it. It took three killers on the loose
from a state penitentiary afore Harmon Adams could actually say what he and I both knew as far back as our
midnight ride to Cavanal Hill the night after Billy Roy
was killed. 'Course I knew it the minute Harmon had put
his arms around me in the doorway of my house that first
Sunday morning. Maybe I didn't know enough to put the
name love to it, but I knew it felt right.

Now here he was out tracking killers, one of them an
Indian who knew what you think an Indian ought to
know about the woods, and the river, and about getting
away from the devil himself. And that Indian probably
would of too, except for the same bad luck that had
turned Falling Eagle into a vicious convict instead of a
noble warrior. The cards were stacked against him.

If he hadn't had the hillbillies, if he hadn't headed our
way, and if he hadn't run into Harmon Adams, who carried a little red Indian blood in his own veins, Falling
Eagle woulda made it. Maybe. His kind, just like Billy

Roy, always seem to follow their own black star toward a bad end.

One of the hillbillies had a cousin in Panama, a little town just a long spit northwest of Poteau, and he convinced Falling Eagle they would be safe there, if they could just reach his cousin's shack south of town.

And they woulda been, too. I hadn't said too much about that side of Oklahoma folks, but just like the Indians, and most of the folks in that part of the country had some Indian in them, them Oklahoma folks were a breed unto themselves. Still are. The dust bowl exodus of the late 30's didn't affect them none. They never farmed anyway. Just did their bit to stay alive one day and got up the next morning to do their bit to make it through another one. When the half-starved farmers left to go to California during the Depression, it just left that much more scrabbling room for those survivors of the area. They weren't all mean or unlawful . . . not all of them . . . but they was all tough as nails.

Harmon Adams passed into legend that day in Panama, Oklahoma, while I was toting a loaded shotgun into the bathroom every five minutes just ten miles away. The radio news kept close watch on the progress of the search and everyone knew the escapees were in the area.

This is the way I understand it, the way Harmon told it to me, and the way I'm going to tell it to you.

It was a cold day—late January usually is in northeast Oklahoma. It was about five, five-thirty. The wind was blowing. Looked like another blue norther headed our way. What sun there had been was setting and the creeks were icing over. Any dog with a lick of sense was at home or heading home toward a fire and a hot meal.

Harmon and his sidekick, a dingy, young, rookie trooper named Joe, were finishing up an unsuccessful sweep outside Panama. They was on horseback and was cold as Eskimos. They stopped at the gas station to see if Idiot Ed had any coffee going. Don't know what they planned to do next 'cause next never came. Sippin' on hot coffee that was more engine oil than coffee beans, Idiot Ed started in telling them about Bad Bill, one of the McAlester State Penitentiary escapees. A local boy.

Well, Harmon knew that. He'd been a rookie himself when Bad Bill had killed his Indian wife on a drunken Saturday night four years before. What he didn't know and what Idiot Ed told him and Joe was that Bad Bill still had kin in the neighborhood. Paul Watts, a cousin, lived just south of town. Harmon didn't know that.

After getting directions, Harmon and Joe headed their horses out Paul Watts's way. It was really dark now and it had started to sleet. They had to turn off the road onto a side one. It was a dirt road, full of water-filled ruts and the horses' hoofs broke through ice with every step. They was almost up to the shack afore they saw it, a pale glow coming through the panes of the one window, and a sleepy smoke curling out of a tin pipe on the roof.

There didn't look like no one was around, but Harmon had Joe hold the horses and he crept up to peek through the dirty window. What he saw inside, caused him to sneak back to Joe and tell him to hightail it back to a phone. Idiot Ed didn't have one, but Harmon thought there was one at the tavern. For him to call the Highway Patrol Headquarters and tell them they'd found the three escapees. He, Harmon, would wait there. Wait as long as he could.

Which turned out to not be long.

Just minutes after Joe rode away, there was a crack of a tree limb on the ground behind Harmon. He heard a curse and then a mutter, "Thought I heard something out here. Well, it's the last time you'll ever come visitin' somebody uninvited, lawman." It was Paul Watts and he shot at Harmon.

And in the gathering darkness, his shot missed. Harmon's didn't.

There was silence in the shack. The fire was put out and the glow from the window disappeared. Harmon could see the smoke from the stove pipe thinning and it soon blackened and faded into the night.

Harmon yelled, "You're under arrest. Come out one at a time with your hands up." I know it sounds like a dime store novel, but what happened out there is where they get the stories for them novels.

These were desperate men and they all three came pouring out of the shack, each firing some kind of gun. Easy targets Harmon said later; silhouetted as they were against the whitewashed shack. He wouldn't have shot at them except they didn't have the same worthy regard for him. With bullets and buckshot flying all around him, Harmon Adams took aim and killed them all. A bullet a man. Even the Indian.

The sheriff and his men . . . I guess you call them a posse . . . hadn't been far away. They had run into Joe halfway into Panama. When they had all headed toward Paul Watts's place, they heard the shooting. They crept up to the clearing and started shining flashlights. Three men were slumped against the shack and Harmon Adams stood over them, his gun still smoking in the cold.

"There's another dead one out here," one of the deputies called when he fell over Paul Watts's body in the woods.

"Well, I'll be goddamned," was all anyone else could say.

Harmon was a real, genuine, honest-to-God hero.

It was late the next morning before I heard from him. Well, there was a phone call. "I'm all right, Bonita Faye. Just cold and tired. I'll be there when I can. I love you."

I put up Billy Roy's shotgun. And laid down on the sofa with an afghan around me. And waited for Harmon Adams.

When he come, he was dirty and smelly and needed a shave. His near-beard rubbed my face raw and his kisses tasted like old coffee, cigarettes, and a little whiskey. We made love for the first time right then and there on my sofa in the middle of the morning the day after he became the hero of the state of Oklahoma.

I never asked him about his soul or how he dealt with killing four men. Just like I never asked him that same question when he was sent home from Korea, wounded, but decorated to within an inch of his life with medals across his chest.

The newspapers called him "a double hero," but all Harmon ever said to me about it was one day when we were walking down one of my favorite country lanes. I was just slogging alone and he was leaning on his cane and he said right out of the blue, "Bonita Faye, I hope I never have to kill anybody again . . . ever."

Bless Harmon, *he* never did have to kill again.

ELEVEN

It was when I was out there in God's country of Glorietta, New Mexico, U.S.A., that I learned how to write postcards. I'd never sent or received one piece of mail in my life and when I was told I had to send a postcard every day back to my mama, it scared me. Who was I to be dealing with the United States Post Office?

Well, sir, they just marched us down to the big hall and made us buy a dime's worth of them penny postcards to send back. Once I got in the spirit of it, I had fun choosing different scenes of Glorietta Baptist Encampment and Surrounding Area. First I sent Mama one that had the Welcome to Glorietta Baptist Encampment sign on it. And then, when I found out they wouldn't get you for it, I began to draw little arrows on the picture side to show Mama, "I was here." Or, "I sleep in this cabin."

The writing side came more difficult. First off I just said, "Mama, the good Lord got us safe here. Amen. Bonita Faye."

I may be slow, but I have never been called stupid,

'cept by Billy Roy and he's dead. And a couple of other times that I didn't pay no never mind to.

Time we left Glorietta I had spent another ten cents on postcards and was virtually scrawling books on the left-hand side reserved for writing.

"Dear Mama, I had fun today. I drawed my sword first in Bible Drill and got another blue ribbon. I'm saving it for to show you with my collection of tree leaves. Did you know every blasted tree has different leaves. All are my favorite. We have Kool-Aid and vanilla wafers every snack. I'm in love with Jimmy Lawrence. So is all the girls. When I'm not having fun, I cry about him. I also love the Lord. And you. Bonita Faye."

I had so much to tell Mama and so little space to do it in that the words were tiny and scrunched up and my signature finally became just a BF way down in the corner, spilling over into the address part. I worried about that. I thought the United States Post Office might get me for writing on their side.

Never having heard of a diary, I was surprised at the reaction I had when I got home and found all my postcards. Mama had tied them together with a piece of packing string and when I untied them the pictures and the words came tumbling into my hands. The days I had spent, the things I had done and the things I had felt all came back to me just like I was there in Glorietta again.

Simple words brought back tastes and sounds. Never again would I ever drink Kool-Aid without a side dish of vanilla wafers. Never again would I hear the wind in the trees without thinking about the individual leaves that sprang from their branches. I think the yearly ritual I've followed all my life of saying, "Thank you, thank you, and thank you" to the changing leaves in the fall started with that trip to New Mexico. To this day I am amazed and feel somewhat guilty about the individuality of leaves on a tree.

Mama knew how much I loved my postcards and she sent me one every chance she could. Now she didn't go

nowhere to send one 'cept once to Mena and once to
Fort Smith. But she'd go sometimes to our very own
post office and send me one right there from home. I still
have them. "Dear Bonita Faye. You are a good gurl. Be
good. Mama."

When I arrived in Paris, France, I thought I was in
postcard heaven. I sent postcards to Harmon off in
Korea, to Patsy and her husband Jerry and their dog
Flop. I sent one to Sheriff Hoyle and his gray-serged wife
Berta. I sent one to everyone who ever nodded "howdy"
to me in my lifetime. I even sent one to Miss Dorothy.
How do you like them apples?

They had postcards of the Eiffel Tower taken every
which way from Christmas and of Notre Dame and, of
course, the *Arc de Triomphe* on the Champs-Elysees.
And they had postcards of pictures people had painted.
Pictures that I could see for real in the Paris art museums.
Imagine having to go all the way to Paris, France, to see
your very first person painted picture.

Every morning I would go down to the sidewalk cafe
around the corner from my hotel and take the stack of
postcards that I had bought the day before on my afternoon tour. I learned to order coffee if it was before noon
and a glass of wine if it was after. I would sip my coffee,
never really coming to like the little cups that Harmon
would have called "panther piss," and I would write my
postcards right there on the Champs-Elysees.

I always sat at the same table and always had the
same waiter. A dark, slender young man in a short white
coat. *"Un cafe,"* I would say. Or, *"Un vin rouge."* I'm
sorry to say that was about it. I could get around Paris,
but as great as it felt being on my own, I was also ham-
pered in what I could do and more importantly eat, because of my lack of the language.

A body could look at those English-French phrase
guides all day, but knowing that *"J'aimerais des
pommes de terre,"* meant "I want some of them potatoes," didn't mean I was going to get them. If there was

a written menu, I'd just point while trying to remember that although fish was *"poisson,"* it wasn't really poison.

It was a funny feeling, being around hundreds of people every day, but never being able to talk to them. I felt like I was in a pharmacist's jellied capsule, closed away from everybody even when I was right in the midst of them. I could see them, hear them, even touch if I wanted to, but they went on with their lives just like I wasn't there. Their conversation and their emotions just swirled around my isolation. Like I had died and some part of me had come back to sit at that white-clothed, sidewalk cafe table in the heart of Paris, France, where I would sit forever not quite knowing what was going on, not quite being a part of life.

My young waiter tried. One day I was so hungry, I just looked at him and said, "For God's sake, please bring me a cheese sandwich before I up and die of hunger." When he just stood there with a frustrated look on his handsome face, I said in desperation, saying more French than I ever had before, *"Fromage. Fromage* with pain."

You could tell when the sun came shinin' through. His brown eyes lit up like dime store candles and he grinned. *"Oh, le croque-monsieur. Avec le jambon?"*

"Jambon?"

"Oui, jambon." He looked around at the other tables, lowered his head to mine and whispered in my ear. "Oink, oink."

We looked in each others eyes, close together because of his previous gesture. Youth and humor won out. *"Oui,* oink, oink. And while you're at it," I added, "I want a Coca-Cola, too."

Coca-Cola is, always has been, and always will be the same in any language.

It was a toss-up, who was more delighted with that first meal I ever ordered in French. Me or the waiter. I had two of them cheese sandwiches with ham. And three Coca-Colas. The bread was toasted, the cheese gooey and more white than yellow, and the ham was paper thin. To this day I have a weakness for *Croque Monsieur*.

As I was brushing away the toast crumbs after finishing my second one, my lovely waiter rushed over and scolded me. *"Non, non. S'il vous plait."* And he whisked out a little bone-handled brush and swept away the crumbs. Then he disappeared into the shop to return with what looked like a long dougnut with gorgeous chocolate on top. *"Le dessert."* It might have been my imagination, but I thought I saw him give a tiny flourish to his presentation of the unexpected treat. He stood beside me, head lowered, while I bit into the fudgey sweet. We both laughed when I was surprised at the first taste of the creamy white center hidden inside. *"Eclair,"* he said proudly.

"Eclair," I parroted. Then, "God, this is good. Thank you, thank you, thank you. Oh, no, I mean, *merci, merci, merci."* I know I said it like, "mercy, mercy, mercy," but he understood. My capsule had dissolved a little. I was in Paris, France. I was sitting at my own table on the Champs-Elysees. I could find food to stay alive. I could make a friend.

He was a little confused when I then asked for *"un cafe."* It was almost like we were back at square one. *"Deux desserts, mademoiselle?"* It was months before I realized the French thought coffee was a dessert, not an accompaniment to one or a luxury to be enjoyed after.

I held my own. *"Un cafe,"* I repeated.

"Oui, mademoiselle." With efficiency, albeit with faint disapproval, he appeared again with a small cup of panther piss.

I pulled out my postcards, selected one with Mona Lisa on the picture side and started a note to Patsy. I had just gotten to the "oink, oink," story when I saw a small gray bug skittering across the tablecloth in search of stray crumbs. My waiter, who had hovered at my elbow, actually looking over my shoulder at what I was writing, was horrified. He reached for his little crumb brush and swept the offender away. We both looked down where it was scurrying away into a crack in the sidewalk. The waiter aimed the toe of his heavy black boot at it.

"No, no. Don't kill it. It's only a little ol' sour bug." I grabbed at his descending foot, throwing him off balance. I just can't stand to see innocent things killed, especially on my account. My young man grabbed at the edge of the table, pulling the cloth half-way off, to keep his balance. *"Pardon, mademoiselle,"* he said with as much dignity as he could under the circumstances as he walked away.

I looked around. It was late in the afternoon and I was the only customer. I gathered up my postcards, wiped the wet coffee off the "Dear Patsy, Jerry and Flop," part of the Mona Lisa one and jammed them into my purse. I pulled francs out of my wallet, even I knew there were too many, and dropped them on the table as I rose.

A finely structured tanned hand appeared on my shoulder, pushing me gently back into my chair. *"Non, non."* My waiter stood there with another cup of coffee. He put it down on the table while he picked up the spilled one and he spoke to me in English, probably the first he had ever said, "I am sor-rey. I am Claude."

TWELVE

If you ever do anything really drastic to change your life . . . like commit murder . . . I sure can recommend a visit to Paris, France, to help you through that time before you reenter the world where people don't commit murder. Now you may not actually be able to get to Paris, or even like the idea of going there, but the important thing is to always have a Paris, France, in your head; a spot that is solely yours—like Paris was mine. A carrot on a stick. A destination that no matter whatever happens to you, you'll be safe there. Some people, I understand, think of heaven in that way.

I first latched on to Paris, France, as my banner for escape when I was fourteen and my stepfather raped me on the dirty, discarded sofa in the Swans' attic. While he was doing his business with me, I rolled my head back over the sofa's edge and looked at a red, white, and blue flag that had the words *Liberté*, *Egalité*, *Fraternité* stitched on it in gold thread.

Later I took Little Alice Swan up to the attic and asked her what the flag was, what the words meant. "Oh, Bonita Faye, I swear, sometimes I think you don't know anything. That's the flag of France and those are the French words for freedom. You stupid girl, don't you know about Paris? The capital of France? That's where they have the kings and queens and everyone is equal. And they have the prettiest women in the world and the handsomest men who all kiss your hand." The little innocent lowered her voice, "And they all drink wine instead of water . . . even the children. And all they eat is chocolate and all they wear is silk."

The next person who dared to call me stupid would die. I hated it when Little Alice knew something I didn't.

When Mama and I left the Swans', it was in the dark of the night so we could sneak away from the no-account Mama had married while I was in Glorietta, New Mexico . . . an unexpected surprise when I got back from Bible camp. Before me and Mama slipped out the back door of the big house, I crept up the back stairs to the attic and took that dusty old flag off the wall, rolled it up around its black stick, and stuck it in the paper sack that was my suitcase. Until Billy Roy gave me my real Paris nightgown, it was the only thing I actually had from France.

Knowing that there was such a place as Paris, France, and thinking about it all the time is a lot different than truly going there.

Not that I didn't like it there. I did. It was just different at first than I had dreamed, but I was some excited when after hours of standing in line in a big gray building that reminded me of the auction barns back home, waiting to go through customs, I finally stood on a real French street with my new suitcase in my hand.

"Taxi, mademoiselle?" A small man with a black cloth beret reached for my suitcase. I jerked the case back and then held it out to him when I saw his taxi at the curb.

In the cab, he turned in the front seat and said a lot of something that I didn't understand. I think he was asking me where I wanted to go. Then it hit me. I didn't know. My game plan had been to get to Paris, France, not to be, in fact, in it.

My driver became impatient and agitated, almost angry. I started to cry and that's when I first learned what softies the French could be. Immediately, he reached a hand out over the seat and patted my arm. He slowed down his speech and finally I understood a word.

"Yes. Hotel. I want to go to a hotel."

The driver said, *"Bien"* which I knew was "good." We smiled. Then he started in again with a bunch of other gobbledy-gook words. I knew he was asking me, "Which hotel?" but I didn't know.

Tears again.

I said the only French words I knew or at least could remember at the time.

"Champs-Elysees. I want to go to the Champs-Elysees."

Again his eyes revealed acknowledgment. Then slowly he asked, "Res-er-vation?"

I was so glad Little Alice wasn't there to know how stupid I was not to have made a reservation. But, then I had never stayed at a hotel and didn't know a reservation was necessary. And I thought how stupid it was not to even know the name of one.

I said again, "Champs-Elysees."

We stared at each other over the front seat for several minutes. Then he nodded and turned in his seat, started the taxi and pulled out into the traffic. He said a lot more of the French words as he made a U-turn, but the only one I understood was "Champs-Elysees." Only he didn't say it quite like I did. I said it like "Elly sees."

There I was Bonita Faye Burnett, in a taxi, in the real Paris, France, driving down the Champs-Elysees, just like I always knew I would.

One of the reasons I knew back then that I was squared away with my soul about Billy Roy's murder is I had heard at Glorietta that God sends angels to protect the innocent and that's no doubt that Denis Denfert was

sent to me that day by Divine guidance, to be my taxi driver and to deliver me safe to his cousin's hotel around
the corner from the Champs-Elysees. Since I was no innocent in any sense of the word, I must have been "made
new" somewhere along the line to receive such blessings
'cause if you're thinkin' that I fit into Paris like a cold
hand in a winter glove then I've left something out.

Could be I didn't explain enough about how tired I
was and that noisy, never-ending plane trip—I had to
stay awake the whole time to keep the plane up in the
air—it didn't help none. And the time change, good law,
it was day when I left America and it was day when I got
to France and nobody ever told me what happened to the
night.

So when my taxi driver's cousin—only I didn't know
that's who he was when he led me into the hotel—took
me to this fancy, high ceiling room, I just fell over on the
bed and didn't move until night had come and gone and
when I woke to sunlight coming through the window, I
thought maybe that was why they called Paris "the city
of lights." That maybe it never was night in France and
why hadn't I read about that.

I still had on my shoes, but someone had covered me
with a white light-as-a-feather quilt which was so snugly
warm that I wanted to close my eyes and go back to
sleep. But a woman in a black uniform knocked on my
door and came on in without so much as a "by your
leave." I hoped she was the one who had covered me up
and reckoned I was right 'cause she acted like she was
trying to take care of me. She had brought in a shiny tray
of what I hoped was coffee, but turned out to be a hot
black liquid that was so dark, thick and bitter that it
looked like it had been brewed from the mud and some
of the weeds that grow down by the banks of the Poteau
River.

"I thank you very much," I told her, "but I'd like some
coffee. If it's not too much trouble."

"Oui, cafe," she said.

I guess that meant I'd have to get up and find a cafe
to get some coffee, so I got up and, after looking around,
found that one of the twelve-foot high doors led to a
bathroom. It was a two-seater, just like back home, but
one of the johns was plumbed wrong. Imagine putting all
that money into a place and then hiring a plumber who
don't know beans.

The lady was gone when I came back into the bedroom and was I some embarrassed. She'd made my bed
and unpacked my suitcase all in the time I'd taken to do
my personal business and slick back my hair. She'd left
the tray though, and I drank the milk from the little shiny
pot figuring maybe they only used glasses for wine in
France—and ate the twisty roll that was wrapped up in
a napkin.

I sat on the side of the bed until I got bored so I got
up and looked out the high window. I couldn't believe
how high I was. At least six floors. Wonder if they knew
airplanes flew this high? Finally I looked down and into
the gray shadows of the street; my hotel and the other
buildings surrounding it kept the sun from shining into
it. I could see a few glassed-in places—shops probably—
and some window boxes full of red geraniums. I wondered how they kept them alive if they never got full sun,
but then on down to the left about a block I could see
real light. And lots of cars.

So this was Paris, France.

Well, I'd come this far, I might as well go see it while
I was here, I thought. I picked up my purse and chose a
door. It led out into the long hall I remembered from the
day before and I walked up and down it for about ten minutes, looking at other tall doors and after a time, not remembering which one was the one that I'd come out of.

I woulda spent my whole first day in Paris in that hallway if I hadn't heard a bell go off and one of the doors
open. Two people stepped out of a little room and the
boy with the round cap acted like he wanted me to come
in. Well, sure, I knew it was the elevator and I got on it.

The lobby was small with a frayed around-the-edges elegance to it; after all it was only a block off the Champs-Elysees. It was about ten o'clock and people with suitcases were coming and going. And the man at the counter was always ringing a little brass bell like he was trying to learn a new tune. Every time he played it, one of the uniformed boys ran forward to see what he wanted.

I went straight to a big over-stuffed chair and sat down. I sat there for four days.

My chair was made of a rough feeling fabric, cross-hatched like a lattice with bouquets of roses growing in the diamond shaped part. It musta been something in its day, but when I sat in it the arms were dark, so stained from the grip of other sitters that you couldn't properly see the original design. And the cushion had been the resting place of so many travelers that it had the trench of their behinds impressed into it—bigger behinds than mine—but after four days, it bore the shallow indention of my shape and I became more afraid to leave it and its comfortable odors and embracing arms.

For a while that first day, I didn't attract much attention. About two o'clock one of the uniforms brought me one of them shiny trays and I took the glass of juice that was on it. I was going to pay for it, but by the time I opened my purse, he was gone.

Wine doesn't taste exactly like Grapette. But some. And, thirsty, I drank it, the sameness of the taste reminding me of the gas station and the cold drinks I'd had there. And I thought of all the times I'd pumped gas between gulps of the sweet drink and of Poteau and . . . even of Billy Roy.

About five the boy came back with another tray with hard bread, milk and more of the hot black drink. Before I could stop him, he poured the milk into the cup with the black stuff and so not to hurt his feelings, I drank it that way. And ate the bread.

About seven, I had to go to the bathroom, so I stood

up, feeling weak, and went to the copper-topped desk. "Excuse me," I said, "I want to go to my room now."

After a hurried conversation among the three men behind the counter, one of them came forward and said, "I speak English. Can I help you?"

"I want to go to my room now," I repeated.

"Are you a guest here, *Mademoiselle?*"

"No, I can pay. But I need to go to my room and I don't know where it is."

"What is your name?"

"Bonita Faye Burnett."

He looked in the book that was a big as a Bible and said, "But of course, Miss Burnett. You're in room 509." And he handed me a key hanging from a brass ball the size of a baseball. "Do you know where the elevator is located?"

"Yes, thank you. I mean, really, thank you."

I showed the new man in the elevator my key and with a shudder that made my stomach dip, he took his little room back to the floor with the long hallway. Only this time I knew my number and used the heavy key to open the door.

Someone had been in the room. They'd unmade my bed and left a piece of chocolate on my pillow. I ate it and drank some water from the bathroom and went to sleep.

The next day, I got to the lobby earlier. I'd had my milk and roll in my room and even had taken a bath. A man was sitting in my chair, but I stood beside it and waited until finally he got up and left and I settled in it, wiggling to reshape the cushion to my backside.

I sat there all day, watching the people, making up stories about them and thinking about Billy Roy. Thinking about when I'd pulled that trigger and wondering if Harmon suspected—if anyone would ever find out. Wondering if I had the strength—I was so tired—to ever get out of that chair and see Paris.

The next day I knew I didn't and that I wouldn't. I

was hungry and felt thinner. Guessed I'd just waste away in that chair and that little guy with the apron would come along and sweep me into that pail that he swept the cigarette and cigar ashes into and dump me outside somewhere.

I drank the wine the boy brought me. And I ate the hard roll and drank what I had decided was the French version of coffee. When it got dark outside, I went back to my room, made supper from the chocolate and went to sleep again.

It was on the fourth day when I realized the uniformed men and the suited ones behind the desk were talking about me. They'd gather around awhile and then all turn to look at me. I smiled at them and they looked away.

Sometime around noon I recognized the taxi driver who'd brought me to the hotel. He was talking to the clerk who had spoken English to me on the first night. I woulda smiled at him if our eyes had met, but he only glanced my way once and left.

After he was gone, the man came from around the counter and headed my way.

"*Mademoiselle*, do you need any help?"

"No, I know where my room is," I answered, but when he kept standing there, I added, "Well, I am hungry."

And he took me by the arm and it was a good thing— I felt as weak as I had when I'd had the poison ivy—and led me into another big room—one where I'd seen people going in and out, but hadn't bothered to find out where they were going. It was full of pink-colored tables and he sat me down at one and snapped his fingers at the white-aproned fellow standing there.

Before I knew it, he brought me a big plate of what looked like yellow sunshine and I ate it; it was eggs with ham in it. And I ate all the rolls and drank milk from a real glass. And when I was finished, the clerk came back and said, "May I join you?"

It turned out that the clerk's name was Thomas and he'd been to the States—Florida. Well, sure, I knew where that was and told him so and that broke the ice.

I told him about always wanting to come to Paris, but that now I was there—here—I didn't know what to do. I didn't speak French and actually didn't even know where to go if I did.

"Well, what had you planned on seeing in Paris?"

"Nothin'. I just always wanted to come here."

"What about the Eiffel Tower?"

"Oh, yeah. The Eiffel Tower," I remembered. "And the Loorve."

"The Louvre," and he pronounced it slowly.

I repeated, "The Louvre," like he did.

"Good. Now, Miss Burnett . . ."

"Bonita Faye."

"Now, Bonita Faye, there is an English-speaking tour that leaves from an office near the Seine every day at one o'clock. Would you like to take it tomorrow?"

"Yes, please."

"Good, I'll call and make a reservation for you. Now you need to go back to your room and rest. You look like you're still suffering from time lag."

"Time . . . what?"

He smiled and his face scrunched up as he tried to find the words to explain in English. "There's a time difference between here and the States. . . ."

"Oklahoma," I interrupted. "Poteau, Oklahoma. That's where I'm from."

"Yes, well, there's a time difference between France and Oklahoma and when you fly here, you pass through these different time zones. Your body doesn't realize it and it gets tired trying to keep up. That's why you've been so tired and . . . and . . . lethargic since you arrived. That and no food. May I take the liberty of ordering your supper to be sent to your room?"

Time lag, I thought that night when I ate the small piece of fish covered with a funny tasting gravy. The waiter had brought it and set it up on a little table right in my room—with a flower in a vase and everything.

Maybe it was "time lag," but more maybe it was that Paris was the stopping point of where I'd been running ever since I'd raced off Canaval Hill. When I'd reached the finish line, I'd just stopped cold. Now with the clerk's help and with aid of the little book I'd found on my bedside when I'd woke up from a really good nap, I could start over . . . start a new race.

I was excited as I flipped back and forth through the pages of what the name said was a French-English—English-French dictionary and phrase book. Did you ever? I asked myself as I looked up the French words for "thank you."

"Mercy" seemed to be the right word for it.

THIRTEEN

*C*laude was my other sign of forgiveness.
There's never been a better friend to any one than Claude has been to me. Except Patsy.

When I finally did leave the Cafe Roy the day Claude brought me my first chocolate eclair, he followed me.

I didn't know it at first.

It's amazing how quickly you adapt to unusual customs. The bicycle riders of Paris had at first fascinated me, but then I got used to them. There were more bicycles passing me on the street in front of my hotel in one minute than there were in all of Poteau and maybe more than in the whole state of Oklahoma. All of Paris moved around on two wheels. The war had been over some years, but with expensive gasoline still in short supply, the real people of Paris still pumped on two legs for their daily bread.

Having grown accustomed to bicycle riders in the street beside me, I didn't pay any attention to the one that coasted along behind me on the way to my hotel. It was when I was starting through the heavy, carved double doors of the hotel, that I heard the low whistle that made me turn my head.

There was Claude leaning over the handlebars of an old bicycle. He'd exchanged his white waiter's coat for a brown cotton windbreaker and his shiny hair hung like black cellophane from beneath a faded beret.

"Oh, hello," I said and turned to approach him.

Claude took off his cap and replied, *"Allo, mademoiselle."*

"Do you live around here?"

"Allo, mademoiselle."

"I'm sorry. I don't speak French."

"I am Claude."

"Yes, I know. You told me. I am Bonita Faye."

"Pardon?"

"Bo-ni-ta Faye."

"Ah, Bo-ni-ta Faye."

"Well, its good to see you. I must be going in now." I didn't move.

"English?"

"American."

"Oui, oui, American. Speak English."

We stood staring at each other. I was reminded of me and Harmon in my kitchen the Sunday morning he came to tell me about Billy Roy. Only Claude and I didn't have any chicken to eat. Suddenly, on impulse, I reached into my purse and pulled out my English-French dictionary. The first part of it is English-to-French, but the back part is French-to-English. I gave it to Claude.

He took it eagerly, so I knew he could read. He fumbled through the pages and looked up and said, "accompany." More fumbling. Then, "picnic?"

"Yes, I'd love to. I mean, *Oui.*" I took the book. With my finger in place on the word, I asked him "when?"

"Ah, demain." I handed him the dictionary again. After a second he said, "Tomorrow." Then, laughing, Claude held up ten fingers, then one. I nodded my understanding. Eleven o'clock. Like my taxi-driving friend

Denis Denfert, he started rattling off lots of words in the language I wish I could speak. He cocked his head to one side in a quizzical pose like a puppy as he spoke as if he was trying to see if I understood any of it.

I didn't.

We laughed in embarrassment.

"Tomorrow, *le livre.*" He pointed to the dictionary.

"*Oui*, I wouldn't dare come without it. *Adios.*" No, Bonita Faye, wrong language. "*Au revoir.*" I turned quickly before Claude saw the pain that slapped my eyes as I spoke the French word for "goodbye." I remembered where I had been the last time I said it.

FOURTEEN

It wasn't just the fun of going on the picnic with a handsome young man at a park in Paris, France. Or giggling over the dictionary that began to fall apart with our constant use of it. Maybe it was the amusement of speaking to each other with our eyes. Certain looks meant, "Do you understand this . . . or that?" "Am I making myself clear?" "Did I say that right?" Maybe it was the satisfaction of getting to know someone different. Or just getting to know someone. Probably it was all of it.

It's excitin' getting to know a new person. It can only happen once to any two people; they start out as strangers and break through a burdensome barrier that, once it has fallen, can never be erected again. At the end of the day Claude Vermeillon and I were friends.

It would be downright tedious to us both if I were to describe to you the stilted, formal, and fractured dialogue we used to get acquainted. So, I'll just tell the gist of it.

Claude was a year younger than me. He was a student at the University of Paris and attended classes from seven in the morning to eleven when he reported to work at his uncle's cafe on the Champs-Elysees. That's why I always saw him there when I came in around one. And he left the Cafe Roy at three o'clock to catch the Metro back to Bois de Boulogne where he lived with his sister, Simone, in the Hotel Regina. Simone was the manager at the hotel that was owned by the same uncle who had the Cafe Roy. If it weren't for relatives, the French would never have jobs.

Bois de Boulogne was its own town located on the same side of the Seine as the Champs-Elysees, miles away from, but easy to get to from Paris; like it is to get to Fort Smith from Poteau.

The French are an emotional lot. When they are angry, it is always to the nth degree and when they are in despair, everyone cries with them. Sympathetic tears ran down my cheeks as much as Claude's when he told of the tragic death of his parents as we sat on one of the Cafe Roy's white tablecloths on the grass by the River Seine. What I didn't understand of his story, I felt.

Now, he said, and his emotions switched again, he was finishing his studies at the University of Paris and he was going to be successful and famous. But most of all he was going to be *"riche-riche."* That meant he was planning to be filthy rich. I thought our communications had broken down, I thought Claude said he was going to make money by buying and selling money. *"Oui."* He pointed to the word in the dictionary again when I questioned him. He was going to buy and sell money to make money. Oh, well, I thought maybe that's what they do in France.

We wiped our tears away with Claude's handkerchief and drank some more wine. Then he said, "You?" in French. I picked up the scattered pages of the dictionary and systematically showed him the words for "father, unknown" . . . "mother, dead." He was sympathetic with these events, but obviously shocked to see me point to "husband, dead." He looked like he might cry again, but when I gave him a dry-eyed look, he didn't. Instead he grabbed the dictionary from me and after flipping through its pages, told me I was too young to have been married. Now, he said, he would call me *"madame."* I told him I preferred *"mademoiselle."*

The next day was Sunday. The cafe was closed so I toured the Louvre again. God, I loved that Winged Victory. Between that and getting lost a couple of times on the bridges crossing the Seine, I made it through the day and even had some fun. I suddenly felt like a Parisian when I sat at a strange sidewalk cafe and ordered *"Croque monsieur"* and they actually brought it to me without any of the usual language hassle. That gave me the courage to buy a red felt beret from a street vendor who helped me put it on, tilting it on my head until he was satisfied it looked right. When I was out of sight of the vendor, I pulled out the red silk scarf I had also bought and tied it around my neck, using my reflection in a shop window for a mirror to guide my efforts. There I was in my white cotton camp shirt, gathered black skirt, cinched at the waist with a wide, red belt and my Paris accessories. God, I thought I looked good. I walked down the Champs-Elysees to my hotel feeling like I was what mama used to call "the talk of the town."

Claude and I played a little game when I walked into the Cafe Roy at one o'clock on Monday. *"Mademoiselle,"* he said pointedly as he seated me at "my" table. He brought me a Coca-Cola without my asking. What fun. What children we were. I ordered my usual "Mr. Sandwich," and Claude presented it to me with an exaggerated flourish.

We met a lot after that. We'd take walks down by the Seine and watch the boats on the river or sit on the dark, damp steps and try to talk without my dictionary. Claude taught me the French words for water and tree. And I taught him happy and good.

"Bonita Faye is a beautiful happy."

"Oui, she is."

I guess we'd agone on forever walking along the Seine holding hands, but one Monday when Claude was pretending to be angry because I wouldn't try something different on the menu, and I was pretending to be angry because he was not bringing me my usual, he jumped and said, "*Oncle* Martin!"

Suddenly Claude and I both felt like the children we had been playing when a tall, stout man in a white apron walked up behind us. Red-faced, Claude introduced me to his uncle who smiled, took my hand and held it while he chattered at me in French. It was Uncle Martin who brought me my order on Tuesday and on Wednesday, when I thought I would never see Claude again, both he and his uncle appeared at my table where I was writing my usual postcards. There was a tiny, gray-haired woman with them. Claude looked excited, but I couldn't tell about what.

"Hello, my dear. I am Mrs. Blount. May I sit down?" the woman asked. In a surprisingly raspy voice, she spoke good English with only a trace of a French accent. Without waiting for my answer, Uncle Martin pulled out the other cane-backed chair at the table for her. He stood over us smiling and nodding. Claude put glasses of red wine in front of us. She went on. "Since neither Martin or Claude speak English, they have asked me to talk to you. To be their translator."

I nodded my understanding.

"I am French," she said proudly raising her chin just a bit, "but I have lived in the United States for the past ten years. Martin Vermeillon and his family are old friends of mine." Her head indicated the two men hanging over our table. "Martin wants me to tell you that no matter what young Claude has said or done, he really is quite a gentleman. Martin wants you to know that he is delighted for Claude to find such a nice young person from America to have as a friend." More smiling and nodding from Uncle Martin.

"Claude's sister, Simone, would like to meet you also.

Unfortunately, her work keeps her away from Paris during the week. So the Vermeillons would like to invite you to be their guest at the Hotel Regina in Boulogne this weekend." Mrs. Blount leaned forward. "I assure you, you will be well chaperoned." She straightened up and turned to the men. "*Alors*. It is settled. Now we will drink our wine, Martin."

Claude and I were going to be allowed to play together after all.

Before she left, Mrs. Blount gossiped to me about Claude's family. I think it was the same story he'd been trying to tell me the day we'd first gone to the park. Since I started studying French words, I might of understood it now, but I was glad that the family's old friend could and would tell it to me in English.

Claude's parents, farmers on some land outside Boulogne, had some kinda link to the French Resistance. For his own protection they had told Claude nothing about their involvement with the underground and it had been a shock to the fourteen-year-old to return home from the market one day to find that his parents had been carted off by the Gestapo . . . along with three British soldiers who were hiding in the Vermeillon's barn.

Simone was working in Paris . . . Mrs. Blount was vague with this information . . . and he had peddled all the way to the city to find her. At the Cafe Roy, his Uncle Martin had not blinked when an exhausted Claude told of the capture of his parents. Instead, he had sent the boy inside for some wine and bread, had taken off his white apron and disappeared. When Uncle Martin appeared again hours later, Simone had been with him. She kissed Claude on both cheeks, clutched him to her breast, and tearfully told him their parents were dead.

Everyone knew the war was going to be over soon. And, in fact, it was only a few weeks later that the French and Americans liberated Paris.

When Mrs. Blount finished the story, I understood why Claude had cried so. Only a few more weeks and

Claude's parents would have lived through the war and maybe have become heroes because of their part in the Resistance. More important, they would have been alive.

After that first time the lack of a translator never bothered me and Claude when we were alone. It just seemed like I knew what he was saying before he said it and he always understood what I was saying. When he stopped by for me after work on Friday, we were so excited we could hardly stand it. When he came up to get my suitcase he nervously wandered around the high-ceilinged room and opened doors and pulled out drawers. Seriously he indicated that the Hotel Regina was not as grand as the one I was staying in, but, and his face brightened, the Regina was clean and comfortable and that he, Claude, would be there. He grabbed my suitcase from the floor and we left after I locked the big white door to my room.

I had walked unnecessary miles around Paris, because I was too scared to ride on the Paris Metro and I couldn't always find a taxi. The subway ride to Boulogne with Claude at my side was easy and I was mad at myself for not trying the subway before then.

As the car rushed and rattled through the dark tunnels, I saw a different side of Paris. Above ground, in the museums, at my hotel and in the restaurants I had mostly seen rich people, the ones who were catered to by folks I now saw riding the subway, men and women dressed in the dark, sturdy clothes associated with hard work. Their faces looked tired and pinched, but as the car raced away from Paris, their workday behind them and a weekend ahead, they began to relax and call teasingly to one another across the aisle.

I think Claude and I came in for our share of the jokes, but I didn't understand and Claude just sat unaccustomedly sullen and silent. When I asked him what they were saying, he just shrugged and said it didn't matter. The subways are faster now, but then it took more than a half-hour to get to Marcel-Sembat, our Metro stop to the Hotel Regina. The aboveground exit literally dumped us out at the door of the Regina.

I loved Boulogne. After three weeks of living in Paris, it was a welcome relief to be in a small town again. Now Boulogne is bigger than Poteau, Oklahoma, by a long shot, but it still has that small town feeling of everyone knowing everybody and all their business. Claude had three people "howdy" him before we walked the few yards to the hotel entrance.

Inside the small lobby, there was a polished cherry-wood registration desk and behind it stood the most beautiful woman I had ever seen. She came around the counter to greet us, taking my face in her hands and kissing me on both cheeks. In heavy accented English she said, "So, this is Bonita Faye. Claude didn't tell me how pretty you are. Welcome to our hotel. We are going to have a good time. *Ooh, la, la.*"

FIFTEEN

Having been a wife and a murderer, I figured I had enough experience in life to know who had been around the block and who hadn't. And Simone Vermeillon had definitely circled the village square a few times in her life. Her face was smooth, white complexion with the same natural high red color in her cheeks that Claude had, and her hair was a shiny blonde, almost white. Her voice was clear and her good manners told me a lot about her dead mother, but it was the pain in her china blue eyes that told me her story.

I saw that same look in my mirror every morning.

While she was welcoming me, saying all the right things for Claude's benefit, our eyes were carrying on a private conversation.

"I see you know me. That's all right. You are welcome here as long as you don't betray me to Claude."

And I answered her in the same silent communion. "Let me be. Let me stay. Like you, I need time to rest. Time to forget. I won't hurt Claude." This exchange was necessary for Simone Vermeillon also knew one when she saw one. No matter how similar or different our sins had been, we recognized one another. We were both survivors. And we both knew what that meant.

The war had altered the course of life for others and I couldn't begin to imagine what dreadful decisions she had been forced to make in a country that was ruled by an enemy. One of those choices was immediately evident. Neither Mrs. Blount or Claude had said Simone was married, but when a young, sturdy boy with pale blue eyes and a shock of blonde-white hair slipped from around the high counter and shied up to Simone's backside, she pulled him close to her and said, "This is my son, Michel." She pronounced it "Me-shell."

The boy was smiling a timid welcome to me when he saw Claude. With a whoop he rushed between his mother and me and jumped into Claude's arms. They were obviously big buddies and had their own established ritual of greeting. Claude swung the boy around in a circle and the toes of the child's scuffed black shoes barely missed hitting me. Then Claude sat the boy down and kissed him on both his flushed cheeks.

"I tell Claude and I tell Claude that Michel is getting too big to climb all over him. Soon Michel will be swinging Claude around." Simone translated to Claude and we all laughed. "Come," she said to me. "Claude will show you your room. Then we will have coffee."

Simone went around the desk, looked through the boxed pigeonholes behind it, and produced a brass key attached to a large porcelain knob. "Number 324, Claude. I am sorry about the stairs, Bonita Faye, but you will be cooler at night if you are up high. I will not worry about you in the daytime. Claude wants to show you many sights. Anyway, it's not so hot this year and a few stairs never bother the young."

When we reached what I thought was the third floor, Claude kept going on up. Then I remembered that Europeans didn't count the ground floor. They just called it "ground floor." Claude was opening the door of room

324 when I caught up with him on what any American would have called the fourth floor.

I didn't have to fake anything to relieve his anxiety about the room. It was small and narrow, painted a blue so deep that it was almost green. A single wooden bedstead, its headboard painted the same unusual color, was in one corner. Next to it was a simple bed stand with a brass lamp shaped like a candlestick. A rose-patterned armchair and chest of drawers completed the furnishings. There was no closet. Instead a row of painted pegs projected from a board on the wall.

I sat down on the white cotton bedspread, my body sinking into the soft mattress. Claude put down my suitcase and crossed to the room's only window and opened it. All I could see was French sky.

"Okay?" he asked.

"Very, very okay. In fact, it's downright *bon.*"

Claude opened the door and showed me that the bathroom was across the hall by miming handwashing. Then he pointed to himself and then downstairs. He held up five fingers. I took it that he would meet me down in the lobby in five minutes. Or at five o'clock. Or in five hours. One of us was going to have to learn the other's language.

After hanging my few clothes on the pegs and putting some underwear in the drawers, I snapped the suitcase shut and shoved it under the bed. Grabbing the heavy key ring, I skipped down the stairs, my hand lightly tracing the smooth wooden railing.

Claude was leaning against the wall in the lobby, his arms folded, one foot crossed over the other. A scowl on his face and tap on his watch meant I had taken too long. I shook my head and held up three fingers. He shook his and held up six. Then we laughed and he grabbed my hand. I looked around for Simone.

"Come," he said after taking my key and returning it to the box.

Ah, English at last.

At the end of the small lobby was another staircase. With Claude pulling on my hand, we bounded down the stairs.

Simone and Michel were waiting for us in the basement dining room. There were flowers, cakes, and cups on one table. Michel pulled his mother's head down and whispered nervously to her. She held his head and said something in his ear, then she pushed him forward a bit.

"It is party," he said in English. "It is Bonita Faye's party."

No one in my whole life had ever given me a party.

While I was exchanging pretty noises with Michel, Simone and Claude were deep in an animated discussion. Still not accustomed to the French way of exclaiming over a pan of dirty dishwater like it was champagne, I was relieved that it was only a discussion of how I liked my room. It made me wonder how excited they would get if a car ever drove through the lobby.

"Claude tells me that you like our van Gogh room."

"Yes, thank you. I do like the room, but who is Vango? Is he a relative, too?"

"No, *cherie*, van Gogh was a famous Dutch artist. He once lived in a little room in Arles, France, like the one you're in. He painted a picture of it and sent it to his brother Theo, to show him where he was living. Now it's a most famous painting and one of my favorites. The room is my impression of how the painting looks. I will find you a reproduction so you can compare."

"I'd like that. I don't know an awful lot about art, but I've sure been learning since I've been in Paris."

After the party, Claude and I walked around Boulogne. Since it was after closing time, we peeked through shop windows and he taught me the French words for the wares sold in each. Then I would say it to him in English.

Supper was served in the dining room downstairs. Some of the other hotel guests were at different tables around the room. A small sign with numbers on it indicated which roomers sat at which table. I ate with the family at the table nearest the door. Everyone knew everyone else and there was lots of talking back and forth between the tables. And, of course, I had to be introduced as Claude's little friend from America to each one of them, even the neighbors who came in for dinner.

Fresh vegetables, cheese, and long sticks of bread made up the meal.

"From Claude's farm," said Claude as he pointed at the potatoes, lettuce, and beans. His English was improving.

"Oh, do you still have the farm?" I turned to Simone for the answer. It coulda been bothersome for her to answer all of our questions and give the answers, but she seemed amused by our company and not to mind the translating.

"*Oui*, the house is burned, but the barn is, how you say, strong. Always we have the garden. It was only food we had in war. Now neighbors do the garden and we share in food and profit. Hotel makes some money, but is not so much. We do many things to make the extra. Everything helps."

It was a wholesome, carefree evening with friends, "family" and lots of laughter in a relaxed atmosphere. I'd never been a part of this kind of experience before and later in my room, as I idly fondled the pink tea rose I had found on my pillow, I wondered why this was so.

Mama had certainly loved me. I had no doubt about that. She had even been affectionate to me in her way, giving me what she could when she had it, and telling me "no never mind" when she didn't. But she had been so busy surviving, keeping me and her alive, that we hadn't had the luxury of the secure, relaxed relationships I'd seen downstairs.

She had taught me to clean, to cook, and to be as honest as she knew how. But, as I had found out tonight, she had cheated us both. Mama had never taught me how to get along when things were good. I had always thought my life took the turn it did 'cause of what that stepman did to me; now I could see that it probably woulda ended up the same way anyhow.

As a natural born survivor—and me being birthed by a lifelong sufferer—we were neither prepared for what to do when the edge we lived on was no longer a dangerous summit.

I wished that she was there with me right then. I'd hug her neck and give her my sweet smelling rose. I'd settle her back in the downy pillows of my feather bed where I could see her tired face in the pink glow of the low wattage bulb in the electric candlelight and I'd say, "Mama, we're safe here. You can stop your running and stop your scrabbling. Come on out of the hen house 'cause there ain't no weasels in France."

Well, Mama was dead, had died and left me with the biggest weasel of them all. But with her training and her instincts, I had known what to do when I had been cornered in the woodpile. Now, on my own, I had to discover what to do when the chicken yard was free of varmints and the gate was left open.

For the first time in my life, I had to decide what to do next based on what I wanted to do, not what I had to do. The first step had been to buy that ticket to Paris, France. I had started to say that it had been when I made love to Harmon in my living room in Poteau the day after he became a hero, but even that act was inevitable. And if there hadn't been no Korea for him to go to, I knew where I'd be right this very minute; in my kitchen fixing chicken fried steak for Harmon, trying not to see the corner of an unused airline ticket sticking up from my orange Fiestaware pitcher.

My coming to France had been my first thought-out, carried-through decision.

SIXTEEN

I decided to stay in Boulogne. It wasn't Paris itself, but since I've always had a cockeyed view of everything anyway, slightly left to center, it wasn't that far off for me.

I asked Simone before I told Claude. I knew who the decision maker was around this place. We were having some of that godawful coffee in the dining room. "So you see, Simone, it would be cheaper and I could stay longer if I made the move here. Besides I love my room and I feel more at home here, more welcome, with you and Claude and Michel. So what do you think?"

I said it that way 'cause I wasn't ready to say, "The Regina feels like home to me. And I want to be a part of a family long enough to know what a family means past just a word I can point to in my dictionary."

"Stay as long as you like, *cherie*. Do what you have to do." Somehow I had known Simone would understand.

My next decisive act was to take my coffee cup over to the serving area and add hot water from the kettle that was always kept going for those who preferred to brew a cup of tea. I took a sip of the diluted French roast and smiled. "Now that's real coffee."

For a Frenchman, Claude was curiously quiet when I told him I was going to stay on. But he was only search-ing for the right words. "Claude is come over," he finally declared. It took me awhile to figure out he was saying he was "overcome," a word I had used to tell Simone how I felt about my van Gogh room.

"And, Claude, I'm gonna teach you English. And you can help me with my French." We had a good system going what with the dictionary and the understanding looks, but who knew what I was missing out on?

Monday morning when Claude went to Paris for school and work, I went with him, to collect the rest of my belongings and to check out of my hotel. The concierge and Thomas, the English-speaking desk clerk were sorry to see me go. At the time, I didn't have the sense to realize how lucky I had been to have Denis Denfert drive me to their hotel. It had been the right choice for me at the time, but now I needed to move on.

With the understanding kindness I have come to ex-pect from the French, they had done their best to make me comfortable and to enjoy their city. Thomas had probably saved my life by giving me food, friendship, and booking me on every English-speaking Paris tour the city had to offer so despite what had been a shabby be-ginning, I had probably had the best introduction to a for-eign country that an ignorant stranger coulda hoped for.

Every morning Denis had picked me up in his taxi and taken me to the tour office where I joined the English-speaking group waiting there. I had boarded my bus, lis-tened to every word the guide said and had followed his red umbrella through every major art museum inside and outside Paris, through the Palace of Versailles, and onto the boats that tour the Seine. I had climbed to the top of the Notre Dame Cathedral and to the bottom of the sewers of Paris.

I had even begun to answer questions for other

tourists when they didn't hear or understand our guide. "What'd he say?" they'd ask.

"He said Montmartre was where St. Denis was beheaded. The man who brought Christianity to Paris. And that's his statue there, the one holding the head." I'd made that tour three times.

The guide acknowledged my help with a smile and a "very good, Bonita Faye." By then I coulda probably got a job with his company if I'd wanted it.

I went by the tour office to tell him I was moving, but that I'd be back to see all my favorite things again with him.

"I will always be happy to see you, Bonita Faye, but I think you could find anyplace in Paris on your own now, especially those on the one o'clock tour." We laughed as we remembered that I'd gone on the one o'clock five times before he'd thought to ask me if I knew there were other English-speaking tours. At ten o'clock, four, and two weekly day tours. I'd taken them all. "Good luck," he said and I knew he meant it.

Claude had written out in French where I was going and why and I gave this message to Denis in our taxi ride back to the hotel. I didn't want him to show up the next morning and find me gone. He would worry about me, or worse, think I was awfully rude not to say goodbye. At the hotel, I tried to tip Denis extra, but he wouldn't take it.

"Nous avons fait un petit bout de chemin ensemble," he said.

I stopped him by holding up the palm of my hand, opened my car door and motioned him to follow me.

Thomas was our interpreter. "Denis is happy to have traveled around with you. The two of you have covered a lot of miles. He wants you to know that he knows of Claude and Simone Vermeillon. When you come into the city, he can be reached at this number and perhaps, sometime he will come out to Bois de Boulogne, if that is agreeable with you."

Well, knock me over. If Denis Denfert knew the Vermeillons, maybe Paris wasn't the big, impersonal city I thought it to be. Maybe underneath, everybody knew everybody else. Just like in Poteau. Come to think on it, I had certainly found my network of friends. For all I knew my taxi driver Denis Denfert might be related to the Vermeillons. Everyone else in Paris was.

I took a long look at him, trying to see what I had missed.

Denis stood patiently on the elegant, but faded carpet of the hotel, enduring my once-over.

He was short, shorter than Claude, and had a deceptively muscular build. Without his cap, which he held in both hands, his dark hair, with gray at the sides, sprang alive. This unruly effect made him appear younger. Lots older than me, but younger than the courtly gentleman I had previously thought him to be. Tiny wrinkles crinkled around his eyes as he smiled. He was actually a handsome man.

Funny how you can see someone every day and never really see them.

I thought of all the kindly things he had done for me. Bringing me to this hotel; he coulda just as easily have driven me to a fleabag or one of the outrageously expensive hotels around the Champs-Elysees. How he had shown up every day, to make sure I was okay, and to see that I arrived safely wherever my destination for the day had been. I had thought it was a coincidence that he was there waiting for me when my tours ended. But, now, I wasn't so sure. Thomas had told me that it was Denis who had sent me the dictionary I'd found by my bed.

I returned his smile.

"Tell *Monsieur* that I sure am thankful to him for helping me all these weeks and I would be proud as punch to see him in Boulogne any time."

Denis Denfert inclined his head in a little bow and whispered, "*Au revoir*, Bonita Faye." And then, surely not, he added, "my little friend." In English.

He was gone before I could make sure.

With Denis gone and my suitcase and extra baggage stored at the hotel desk, I wandered into the *Tabac* store next door to buy more postcards and stamps. I wanted to send Harmon and Patsy my new address and explain why I was moving out of Paris. Not that it would make them no never mind. Boulogne or Paris meant as little to them as wherever it was that Harmon was in Korea meant to me. You may have noticed that geography was not a strong point for people from Oklahoma. I coulda written that I was going to Chiny and Patsy woulda thought it was next door to Paris.

It was me she cared for, not where I was.

Patsy was a "blank check" friend. One of the ones you could give a signed blank check to and trust not to wipe out your bank account.

We'd met each other at church in Poteau. As one of his public relations efforts, Billy Roy had insisted we join a church. Since I had gone to Glorietta and all, I always thought of myself as Baptist, so we wound up one Sunday morning joining the First Baptist Church in Poteau. That was the only time Billy Roy stepped foot in it, 'cept when they carried him in feet first. But he made me go every time they opened them church doors.

I kinda liked it though. Especially the Ladies' Bible Study. We'd meet in different one's homes and have a little prayer, and a little Bible verse study, and a little something to eat. The women would always try to outdo themselves and cook up their special desserts. Berta would fix her German chocolate cake which was different than Ethel's American chocolate cake. I don't need to tell you what Miss Dorothy made when we met at her house. And I took to fixing the Eagle Brand lemon pie my mama had taught me how to make.

It got where I could say "howdy" to the Baptist women when I saw them at the market, or wave to them if I was swinging on my front porch and they passed by in their big cars. And since I could read so well, it got where they always asked me to read the Bible verse of the day at the monthly meetings.

There was a kinda peckin' order to church. The banker and the mayor and such and their wives sat right up front. Right under the preacher's eyes so they could be sure to be counted on the rolls up yonder. Not knowing where I fit in, I moved around a lot to the different pews. That's how I found Patsy. She always sat perched on the very back pew, like at any minute, she might bolt and run out the door.

I noticed her first 'cause she seemed about my age. Maybe a bit older. Lord, 'cept for Claude, it seemed everybody I knew was older than me.

It was on a Sunday that I hadn't wanted to go to church, but I hadn't wanted to stay at home with Billy Roy more, so I slipped in late, and sat in the back by this woman who always was there in church, but I didn't recall just who she was. I recognized her not only from her pew position, but also from the plain navy blue dress she always wore. She was sitting slumped forward a bit, her eyes on the folded hands in her lap. Her long straight black hair that was normally tied in a ponytail at her neck, fell loosely around her face.

She didn't look up and greet me like most people did and I was glad of that. However, I could feel her looking at me when she didn't think I was looking. When the music director signaled for the congregation to stand and sing Hymn Number 148, we stood up at the same time and our hips bumped. Instinctively, we both looked up to react and apologize, but what we saw, caused us both to burst out laughing.

We both had beauts of shiners; her on her left eye and me on my right. Our laughter was just barely covered up by the organ prelude to the hymn, and, in fact, a little boy in front of us turned around to stare, first 'cause of the noise, then 'cause of the black eyes.

Have you ever started laughing at something and know you're never going to be able to stop? Well, Patsy and I did that all the time, and the first time was that Sunday. Before the last verse of the song, we both pretty much had figured out what was happening to us and before the congregation sat down again, we had sneaked out of the church.

Outside, it was Sunday morning calm. You could smell the fresh cut churchyard grass and birds were everywhere, singing or searching for bugs in the newly disturbed yard. Patsy and I leaned up against the white columns of the church to catch our breaths.

I regained my composure first and defensively said, "I got mine running into the clothesline."

Patsy simply said, "My husband hit me."

She was more honest than me and we both knew it.

And then she laughed again, and I got my second glimpse of the humor with which she viewed the world. "But, I hit him back and he's got two of these."

We never spent another day apart from that time on until I went to Paris, France.

Patsy couldn't read a word if her life depended on it. She wasn't a dropout like me, she had never even been to school. I hadn't seen her at the Ladies' Bible Study 'cause, to them, she didn't exist 'cept to come in their back doors to collect or return their ironing.

She had lots of Indian blood in her, but somebody along the way had given her bright turquoise eyes. That was about the only truly beautiful physical feature she had, but someone, maybe God, had also given her the serene, easygoing attitude that enabled her to cope with her lot in life. She had married Jerry when she was thirteen and had six kids already. A naturally loving mother, she nurtured those kids like a bitch hound nurses its pups. They were free to roam and do whatever they wanted long as they showed up to be counted, hugged, and fed ever so often.

And Jerry was the best no-account man I ever met.

Not much better educated than Patsy, he did all the odd jobs around town, showing up in his clean, starched and ironed overalls to paint houses, fix shutters, the roof or the plumbing. He was the one who cut the grass at church.

And he loved his Patsy. And their kids. When he hit her, he did 'cause of the background and upbringing they were both used to and nothing personal was intended. And when he hit her, she just hauled off and socked him back twice as hard and twice as much. That didn't make it right, but it worked for them.

Patsy was so smart that she had memorized what she couldn't read. She knew the whole Bible from cover to cover.

One day, soon after we met, we were in my kitchen, drinking coffee, eating chocolate chip cookies, and talking about religion, and I told her about Glorietta and about me speaking out from behind the bushes. It was the only Bible verse I had ever memorized, so I showed off a little, and recited it to her.

"Well, now, ain't that good, Bonita Faye. Only that ain't all of it, you know."

"I don't follow you, Patsy. What ain't all of it?"

"The rest of that part you recited to me. The next part goes like this:

"And he said unto me, 'Write, for these words are true and faithful.'

"And he said unto me, 'It is done. I am Alpha and Omega, the beginning and the end. I will give unto him that is athirst of the fountain of the water of life freely.

'He that overcometh shall inherit all things; and I will be his God, and he shall be my son.

'But the fearful, and unbelieving, and the abominable, and murderers, and whoremongers, and sorcerers, and idolaters, and all liars, shall have their part in the lake which burneth with fire and brimstone: which is the second death.'"

I was some impressed.

SEVENTEEN

My days at the Hotel Regina took on a pleasant sameness.

I got up late every morning and enjoyed a continental breakfast in the basement dining room: a fresh croissant and watered-down coffee which, I don't need to tell you, drew considerable contempt from the Europeans who ate there, but I felt justified when the few Americans who had found their way to the outskirts of Paris nonchalantly began to imitate my teapot habit. Like me, they had even started bringing the unused shaving mugs placed in each room for their "Americanized" coffee.

"You just can't expect Americans to drink thick, French roast coffee out of those little ol' things," I told Simone. "Yes, our coffee is watered down, but, look at it this way, we drink twice as much so you can charge twice as much for it."

"I'll never understand," she replied. But I did notice that the shaving mugs began appearing on the white-clothed, breakfast buffet table next to the demitasse cups.

Boulogne has attractive parks and its own interesting history and for awhile I enjoyed wandering around, finding my way through the town. The hotel was shaped like a flatiron with its pointy end spilling into a traffic circle that led off onto six different streets: one led to the post office, another to the *hôtel de ville* and another to the park. I explored them all, stopping in to poke around the surrounding shops as I went.

One day I came across a small bookstore that had an intriguing message printed in black letters in the corner of one its display windows. It said "American Literature." I pushed open the door and entered.

Inside, I found my fifth best friend.

Mama was my first, Patsy, my second. Harmon counted as number three and Claude, fourth. Simone and I weren't there yet, so Robert Sinclair got to be fifth before she did. Or Denis Denfert.

In my best French, I said, "Pardon me, can you tell me the meaning of the sign on the window? American Literature?" My best obviously wasn't good enough, 'cause the tall one-armed man standing there didn't respond. Frustrated, I repeated my question, louder this time.

"Sure can. No need to shout. Means I'm the only one in Boulogne who sells books written in English." Not only did he reply in English, but it was with an American accent. Different from mine, but still American.

"Then why didn't you say that the first time?" I asked irritably.

"I was trying to decide what it was you were saying."

"Well, I know my French isn't very good, but . . ."

"Good! It's atrocious. You shouldn't be speaking it. You should be grateful that the French haven't sent you to the guillotine."

"What's wrong with the way I speak it?"

He rubbed the side of his long nose with the stub of his left arm which ended at the elbow. "You speak French like an Arkie. Am I right?"

"Okie," I corrected and then admitted, "Well, maybe

some Arkie. I'm Bonita Faye Burnett from Poteau, Oklahoma."

"I know who you are. You're the young woman who's staying with the Vermeillons at the Regina. I'm Robert Sinclair from Media, Pennsylvania. I was hoping I would have an opportunity to meet you."

I was flattered. "Oh, because we're both Americans?"

"No, because I want you to leave young Claude alone."

Now Claude and I were best friends and maybe, I suspicioned that he was courting me some, but I hadn't thought our private relationship had reached the level of street talk. I stammered, "What do you mean?"

He pointed the index finger of his only hand at me. "You're the one who has been teaching him English. I want you to stop it. You shouldn't even be speaking English. Or French. Your ignorance will ruin him."

I flushed red. Tears stung my eyes. I ran out of the store. I don't think I've ever been so embarrassed and so angry at the same time.

The nerve of that man. The gall. Who in the hell did he think he was?

I finally stopped my pell-mell rush though the streets. Taking my bearings, I headed for the park, and walked through the marked paths until I came to the waterfall. Going as close to the edge as I could, I stopped and stared at the cascading water.

I'd leave Boulogne today. I wouldn't even say good-bye to Claude or Simone. I'd leave Paris. France. I'd go home where I belonged.

How dare that man call me stupid.

I hated being called stupid.

As my breathing returned to normal, so did my thoughts. A small voice inside me said, *Now hold on Bonita Faye. He called you ignorant, not stupid. There is a difference. And you are kinda ignorant. You didn't graduate from no high school and you do talk like a hillbilly.*

It musta been about an hour later when I walked back

into Robert Sinclair's bookstore. I carried a box with two chocolate eclairs and two paper cups of coffee. French coffee. I waved my treat in front of him. "Can we start over?" I asked.

This time Robert was the one with the red face. "I'm sorry. I get carried away. I didn't mean to be so blunt. Is that supposed to be a peace offering? If so, I should be offering it to you. I would have come after you, but I couldn't leave the store open. By the time I locked up, I couldn't tell which way you had gone." His words tumbled out, one steppin' on the other. "In short, yes, let us start over, Bonita Faye Burnett from Poteau, Oklahoma."

He brought a brown leather-topped stool around the counter and sat on its mate on the other side while we had our strange tea party, peace talk.

After telling Robert my story, well, most of it anyway, he pushed back our paper trash and said, "Let me get this straight. You haven't had much formal education, but you enjoy reading and, as a matter of fact, seem fairly well read."

"And I wouldn't hurt Claude for nothing," I added.

"And you wouldn't hurt Claude for anything."

"What should I do, Robert?" We were on a first name basis by then. "Should I leave France? Go home?"

"Let me think about it. I have a half-formed idea in the back of my head, but give me tonight to work on it. I know Claude and Simone care about you or they wouldn't have wanted you to stay on. In the meantime, until tomorrow, don't do anything different. And, right now, I want to ask you some questions."

"Like a test?"

He laughed. "Yes, that's right. Like a test."

It wasn't like no test I'd ever had in school. Instead we just talked books. I told him what I'd read and where I'd got ahold of the books. And about my obsession with Paris, France. Only not why.

We even argued about what I liked to read. I found myself defending my favorite fictional best friend, David Copperfield.

Davey was like a brother to me.

See, I never knew, still don't, if rich people are clean . . . or clean people are rich. Whichever it was, I only knew that they wanted my mama to come and cook and clean for them. And that having a skinny little ol' daughter with her didn't matter to them or to Mama.

I didn't take up much room, was quiet as a mouse, and lived mostly with the thoughts in my head. Mama and me fit good together in the usual single bed off everybody's kitchen. And it was comforting to both of us to know the other was nearby. Mama would be frying the chicken-fried steak in the kitchen and mixing up the best dog-trot gravy in the county, and I would be snuggled up in what folks call "the maid's room" with a book that I had sneaked from the library. I always returned them like I found them, clean and shiny, with the only thing being different was that now they had been read.

Besides being clean, another thing rich people have in common is they always had the "Great Works of the Masters" somewhere in their house. It got so that when-ever we moved, which was a lot—someone was all the time offering Mama another dollar more a week—that the first thing I'd look for was the Great Works like them books was a sign that even though the curtains might be green instead of blue in this house, someone I knew was waiting for me. Waiting to say, "howdy, Bonita Faye," and "welcome home."

And Davey Copperfield was my favorite.

"So you see, Robert, David wasn't no great shakes as a person. It was the people around him who led him by the nose. Or more rightly, the people Charles Dickens put around him. Poor ol' Davey just did what them others told him to. The sucker never had an original thought in his own head. Why, he never did know what came next without someone telling him! It amazes me that he got through life."

"Hmmm, interesting train of thought, Bonita Faye. Well, I think that about does it for today. I have some paperwork to do this afternoon. Can I expect to see you here, hmmm, about nine o'clock tomorrow morning?"

"Yes, sir. I'll be here." There weren't, and still aren't, many people I call "sir."

The short of it was that Robert Sinclair became my teacher. Of both English and French. And I added him to my growing "friend list."

The long of it was that he taught me so much more than language skills.

That first morning he gave me a gift that's stayed with me all my life. The gift of myself. "Bonita Faye," he said right off, "I am giving you permission to use what you already know." When I said, "that ain't much," he shushed me and went on. "I beg to differ with you. You've read a great deal of very good literature. On your own volition. That says a lot about your character and your determination.

"Now, I'm giving you permission to use what you've read. You know correct English because you've read it. With practice you can speak it." He paused and smiled. "I don't think we'll ever be rid of that accent, but that's all right, too. It's a part of the important person who is Bonita Faye Burnett."

"She ain't so important," I said.

"Yes, she is, too. Extremely important. And, as you let her through that wall you've put around her, I think you'll find her an interesting person, also. But, Bonita Faye, don't ever let me hear you say 'ain't' again. Is that clear?"

"Yes, sir," I said, but the old Bonita Faye in me wanted to argue that Mark Twain had Tom Sawyer saying "ain't" all the time and I wasn't too sure I didn't remember the forbidden word in some of Dickens's work. For the time being though, I held silent.

I was some embarrassed when I began to realize that Claude and I had been talking to each other like Tarzan and Jane. "Me come here. You park go." And, "Me like you."

"That's all right, Bonita Faye," Robert said when I cried over this discovery. "That's called communication. Or the beginning of it, anyway. It's not what you've done before that's going to be a problem for you. It's what you're willing to do now."

Claude laughed when I told him about Robert Sinclair helping me to learn to speak correctly. Only Claude thought it was just French I was learning. Robert and I decided Claude didn't need to know about the English part. "That's between you and me, Bonita Faye. Don't worry, I'll take care of the few inappropriate English phrases you've taught Claude. That boy has a fine future ahead of him. Something he probably wouldn't have been able to accomplish before the war."

He paused to see if I was following him. "That's why I was so upset by your teaching him fractured English. Claude must only speak the best. France doesn't have the structured class differences that the English have, but before the war, it would still have been difficult for Claude to achieve his goals. Now with his education at the University of Paris, Claude can do or be anything he wants."

"I think he wants to buy and sell money," I told Robert cautiously. I didn't want him laughing at me. "Does that make sense to you? Or is it another example of how poorly Claude and I have been communicating?"

Patiently, Robert explained the international financial market to me. I didn't quite grasp it, but then, like I've always said, numbers aren't my friend. But if Robert and Claude understood that there was profit to be made in exchanging money from one country to another, and it was legal, then it was okay with me.

What I did understand and, what Robert taught so beautifully that it seemed just like conversation, was a lot of history mixed in with the language lessons. I found out that the French flag wasn't red, white, and blue, but *blue, white, and red.* That the French Revolution had come after the American one. When I blinked blank on that, Robert had stopped and explained our own country's revolution. I didn't know we'd even ever had a *king*. Think on that.

When I asked him what he was doing in France himself, he said, "This is where I was stationed during the war. I was an American liaison with the French Resistance. This is where I fought. Where I lost my arm. And . . . found myself . . . like you're doing now.

"After the war, I went home to Pennsylvania and taught for awhile at the university, but I felt like I belonged here. So I came back. I guess you could say I left my heart and soul here. And, of course, my arm. Now I feel complete."

I understood that explanation. I knew all about being at peace with your soul.

EIGHTEEN

I didn't become a college graduate overnight, but after practicing the tricks Robert taught me, even I could tell my English was improving. And they were just tricks. Things like remembering to pronounce the "ing" in words that use it, watching out for double negatives. And pronouncing words correctly, like the "cog" in recognized. And I didn't ever say "ain't" again.

At least not in front of Robert or Claude.

When I talk about my beginnings, about home, or get sentimental in some way, I hear myself slipping back into the old ways which are as comforting to me sometimes as a pacifier is to a baby. I know that's how I've told more than half this story, but that's all right 'cause that's part of my being Bonita Faye.

And Robert Sinclair taught me that being Bonita Faye is okay.

Now when I went into Paris some mornings with Claude, I retraced my steps and took the same tours all over again. My old guide would roll his eyes and say, "Oh, no, not you again. Remember, Bonita Faye, this is my tour and my job to tell the tourists what they're seeing, not yours." But he would smile when he said it.

This time when I toured, I really listened and with Robert's help, the history part started coming alive for me. I liked the Revolution years the best. Imagine going from the legacy of the Sun King to the gore of the guillotine. There's a case of your best plans going awry for you.

My French improved and with Claude taking English lessons from Robert also, he and I were finally able to speak to one another like we wanted to.

I'm afraid now that I've got to go back and confess that most of Claude's story that I said he told me that first day was really told to me by Mrs. Blount when she came to translate the Vermeillons' invitation to me. I had understood his account of his life and of his parent's death, had actually felt his grief and wept with him, but Mrs. Blount was the one who sorted out the story for me. She and I continued to meet occasionally at the Cafe Roy for a glass of wine and conversation.

"You've changed, Bonita Faye. I can't quite put my finger on it, but you have definitely changed since I first met you. You're prettier and more interesting. It must be the country air." And since she was an old die-hard romantic at heart, she leaned in close to me, like she liked to do when saying something personal, and added, "Maybe, *cherie*, maybe it is our Claude. Ah?"

Ah, indeed, I thought to myself. You sweet, nosy, busybody.

It was no secret to me that Claude was the one who left the fresh rose on my pillow every night. Or that his brown eyes turned a golden amber whenever he looked at me. I had never been courted before and I went along with it, innocent like, just to see where this experience would lead. Into the bedroom, I figured. Not that all of me would mind. I hadn't been a virgin in some years and always had enjoyed sex unless it was forced on me. Even with Billy Roy when his eyes were shining nice. And it seemed like an awful long time since I had said goodbye to Harmon.

When Denis Denfert made good on his promise to call on me in Boulogne, I was surprised to see the same bright lovesick gleam in his eyes. For Simone.

The two of them had acted like polite old friends, meeting again after an absence of some years. But there were some things they did that told me they were better acquainted than their actions indicated. Like Simone telling me to set out the white wine instead of the usual red, "because Denis prefers it." Or Denis looking Simone square in the eye when he said, "Michel is a fine boy, Simone. You have done well by him."

Was it possible that Denis was Michel's father?

Denis stayed a long time after supper was over. He and Simone were drinking the white wine and making polite conversation, but both Claude and I got the feeling they might want to be alone, so after drinking our share, we said good night.

My real, real Paris nightgown was nothing like the one Billy Roy had got me. It was made of white cotton muslin with small straps and a shallow yoke from which yards of gathered material fell to an even fuller ruffle around my ankles. I had it on, holding the red rose I had found on my pillow when I heard a knock at the door. Of course, it was Claude.

He came in and took the rose and held it to his lips. Then he slowly began to trace a gentle pattern over my arms with the flower. His eyes shown a golden honey color as he moved the rose slowly up to the hollow of my neck.

"Claude," I said in weak protest.

The French language is not called a romance language for nothing. Claude whispered touching and embarrassing words as his lips began to follow the path of the rose.

I'd like to tell you that I stopped him. That I said "no" as tenderly as I could. That he stopped and quietly left the room.

And maybe I did and maybe he didn't stay with me.

The years go by and what really happened and what I imagined might not be the same.

I can nearly believe to this day that I can feel his strong, slender body against mine. Having been used to bigger men—Harmon towered over me—it was a shock to feel a man's body pressing against mine on an equal level. Although Claude's legs were longer than mine, I didn't have to stretch to wrap my arms around him and he didn't have to bend away from me to kiss my lips.

I can almost remember that we became lovers that night.

But surely we didn't.

I wasn't that far into being independent and making my own decisions, and I wasn't all that sure that accepting Claude as a lover was one of the choices I wanted to make. For one thing, I wasn't clear how I felt about Harmon. He was a good man. I was grateful to him for reasons he'd never know and for some he did. I felt protected by him. Liked making warm love to him. He'd said again, "I love you, Bonita Faye," before he'd left for Korea. And I'd replied, "I love you, too, Harmon."

Surely that wasn't me making love with Claude. Surely it's just in my memory that I stood in my van Gogh room in France and whispered, "I love you," to a man . . . and in a language . . . that I hadn't known six months ago.

How could I be expected to make the right choice when it was obvious that I wasn't even sure what love was?

NINETEEN

"They told me you were dead." It was a combination of the strange words and the recognition of the desperate voice that uttered them that made me turn my head toward the speaker.

It was Simone.

We were seated at a sidewalk cafe in Paris, not the Cafe Roy, but one near the tour office. I had stopped for something cool to drink before going on to meet Claude for the trip home.

Simone was sitting at the table in front of mine. She must have been seated there when I arrived, but the large brimmed black hat she wore kept me from noticing her until I heard her voice. The same big hat brim kept her from seeing me behind her as she nervously glanced around.

I could see her companion clearly, the one she was surprised to find alive. He was a big man, good-looking in a blonde way, with intense blue eyes that never wavered from Simone's gaze. He looked vaguely familiar. I couldn't hear what he was saying, but it apparently upset

Simone. She kept saying, "No, no," to him. He reached over and grabbed her wrist and held it down on the table between them. While I was focused on the hand that held Simone's, she wrenched it away and stood up. Her abrupt turn put her in front of my table where she stared at me through tear-filled eyes. With a gasp and a quick look at the other table, she turned again and ran away.

I looked over at her former tablemate.

He sat still, his eyes on Simone's retreating figure. He didn't see me at all. He had mean eyes. Now I knew who he reminded me of. Billy Roy.

It was late that night before I had a chance to be alone with Simone. She hadn't appeared until supper and then ate with unusual apathy. Michel was the only one who claimed her attention, but before she could leave the table with him, I reached over and said, "Simone. Look at me. I want to talk to you. Come back after you put Michel to bed. I'll wait here."

You could tell she didn't want to, but finally, she nodded and took Michel by the hand.

I watched the night help clear away the dishes. Claude had already spread his books and was deep into his studies. "Claude, can you do that . . . study . . . in your room tonight? I need to talk to Simone. Just girl talk. You'd be bored and besides we would interrupt your concentration."

He gathered up his books, gave me a tender kiss behind the ear and left.

It was almost an hour before Simone returned. While I waited I turned over in my mind the relationship Simone and I had developed over the weeks I had been staying at the Hotel Regina. Wary and suspicious myself, I had been thrown for a loop when Simone had opened her home to me . . . well, I was a paying guest . . . but the way she included me in everything, you'd never have known it. I always sat at the family table and was introduced as a family friend. And the way she trusted me to watch after her son and the way she had practically given me her brother.

The alliance Claude and I were cultivating was supposed to be secret and our own business. But, in France, as in Poteau, everybody knew your personal matters almost as soon as you did yourself. Only in Poteau, they went, "*tsk, tsk*," and pointed fingers. In France, they smiled and said, "*c'est la vie.*"

Simone never gave me any indication that she approved or disapproved of the flirtatious romance Claude and I were pursuing. Instead when she came upon me sitting in the lobby about the time Claude was due home, she would smile and raise her eyebrows. "I don't need a clock to tell me it is time for our Claude." And she brought a cardboard hat box to my room and said, "For your dried roses, *cherie.* I will show you how to make a potpourri from them." She knew who had been leaving me those roses.

She did deplore my wardrobe, however. My plain full skirts, camp shirts, and blue jeans did not meet with her approval and she was brutally honest about it. As honest as Robert Sinclair. "Bonita Faye, Claude tells me you have been married? Yes?"

"That's right, Simone." The way she looked, I thought she was probably going to throw me out of the hotel.

"Then, my love, why do you continue to dress like a little girl? Anyone who has experienced the thrill and passion of being a woman in love should not cover her body with schoolgirl clothes."

I didn't correct her, didn't tell her that it was ignorance on how to dress rather than a denial of my womanhood that dictated my wardrobe. And that the only thrill and passion of romance I had ever known was from her brother when he crossed the hotel hallway from his room to mine every night. Instead, I said, "You're right, Simone. What can I do to look more grown?"

"That is no problem. You are fortunate that you are living in Boulogne, only a few short miles from the *haute couture* capital of the world. If you are willing, I will help you."

You couldn't even tell where Patsy had sewn the collar back on my yellow two piece from Fort Smith, Arkansas, after Billy Roy's funeral. It was the only dress I owned that Simone thought was halfway acceptable so I put it on and we went to Paris to scout out the famous stores on Avenue Montaigne.

"I don't think I can afford one of them dresses from that Montana street," I told her on the subway.

"No, no, Bonita Faye. No one buys them. One copies them. Like I do."

So that was how her slim, attractive body was always clothed in dresses that were tucked just right at the waist or flared seductively at the hemline. Even her around-the-hotel workdresses were made of swirling floral patterns and she always changed into chic ensembles for supper with the guests.

To my surprise we didn't go in any of the fancy stores on Avenue Montaigne. We sat on a stone bench on the median that divided the wide street. "Why don't we go in?"

"Do not be silly, Bonita Faye. Designer dresses would do us no good unless we are going to have dinner with the president or enjoy a show at Maxim's. Look. That is what we want to see." Simone indicated a group of three women about to enter Christian Dior's gray building. A uniformed doorman bowed and opened the door for them.

"French designers are trying so hard to make up for the ground they lost during the war, that they are not designing clothes for the real women of France. I do not know if Paris will ever be the *haute couture* king again, but, the women who shop here know how to dress. It is them we watch and it is their dresses we copy," Simone explained.

We had fun, eyeing the customers and admiring or criticizing their outfits. When Simone decided she knew enough about my likes and dislikes, we went to a small fabric store near *Galeries Lafayette* and picked out material for two new dresses.

On the way home, I told her how much I had enjoyed the day and how much I appreciated her helping me. Her blue eyes that never seemed to darken, widened. "But, my friend, I am the one who has enjoyed the day. Since the war, I have lost touch with my old friends . . . women friends, and like Claude, I find you refreshing and honest. I never had a sister, *cherie*, and men have always liked me more than women, but I think we get along well enough, you and I. We are becoming friends, yes?"

It wasn't the same as with Patsy, but I also enjoyed the easygoing companionship between Simone and me. We laughed as we measured and sewed my new clothes. Not gut-busting snorts, but enough so we wiped away a few tears. Especially when Simone told me stories about Claude as a youngster or like on the day she taught me to wear high-heeled shoes.

I had noticed from my time sitting at the Cafe Roy that all French women wore high heels—without stockings—and their calf muscles were strong from the constant walking they were required to do every day. My legs looked spindly and fragile in the new shoes. "I can't walk in these, Simone. I'm gonna fall over," I protested.

"Practice, practice, practice, Bonita Faye. By the time this dress is finished, you'll be able to manage a decent walk. Don't women walk in Oklahoma?"

"Not on spikes."

Together we explored the shops in Paris and Boulogne, looking for just the right trim or accessory for my new outfit. That's how I got to see even another side of French life and how, slowly, Simone and I became friends.

Michel often accompanied us on our excursions and he and I became almost as big of pals as he and Claude. When we would reach the hotel after a day's shopping, Simone would rush to get ready for the supper crowd

and I'd often bathe Michel or play quietly with him until
we ate. He'd sit in my lap and eat cookies and milk and
I'd brush his hair back from his eyes and give him a kiss
on his temple like I did Patsy's kids back home. I could
taste the salt from the perspiration that gathered on his
forehead. The feeling I had for Michel came from deep
inside and swelled my heart. I wondered if I could love
him any more if he had been my own. I wondered what
it would be like to be a mother.

Simone invited Robert Sinclair to supper when my
new dress was ready. Like it was a party. I came down
the stairs to the dining room slowly, but balancing well
on my new shoes.

Both Claude and Robert gave me appreciative looks,
then Claude's brown eyes darkened.

"What's the matter?" I whispered to him when I
slipped into my seat beside him. "Don't you like my
dress? Is there something wrong with it?"

"Before only I knew the woman inside. Now everyone
can see. I liked you the way you were." He was jealous.
Simone and I exchanged knowing looks. My dress was
a success.

I was wearing it the night I waited for her to put Michel
to bed, absently smoothing one of the pink-flowered
flounces, waiting for her to return and tell me what had
happened that afternoon in Paris when the stranger in
the cafe had upset her, when her voice startled me.

"Bonita Faye, I don't know what you imagined you
saw today, but it wasn't what it seemed."

"You don't know what I imagine and, believe me, I
have a pretty active imagination, but I didn't misunder-
stand what was going on. Who is that man, Simone? And
why are you afraid of him?"

Simone began a denial which disintegrated into a sob
as she sank into the chair next to mine. "I don't want
Claude to know. I have hidden it from him for so long.
Promise me, you won't tell Claude."

"I'll promise I won't tell Claude as long as I can keep

from it. But, not if I think he can help you. If it's that serious, he may have to know, Simone. Claude's a man and he may be able to take care of the matter for you." You can see where I was in my thinking. Even with my background, I still thought it took a man to fix a problem.

"But, Bonita Faye, that's exactly why Claude should not know. He will try to kill Max and Max is stronger, bigger." Simone's accent became more pronounced as her agitation grew. "I am afraid Max will kill Claude."

"Hush, hush. Calm down. Now who is Max? And what does he want from you?"

She looked as though she thought she didn't have any choice. She told me. "Max is Michel's father."

Not Denis Denfert.

"It was in the war. You notice, we don't speak of that time much here. It is too painful. Our parents dying. The farm destroyed. Claude was so young then. It was easy to lie. Even so, he always thought Michel's father was my great French lover who died fighting in the Resistance during the last days."

"And that's not true?"

"No, no. I thought you recognized. . . . That you knew."

"What, Simone?"

"That Max is German. That Michel's father is a German."

I do not approve of taking the Lord's name in vain, but when Simone divulged Michel's paternity, I said, "Jesus Christ!"

"Exactly, so you see . . ."

"But I thought women who . . . well . . . I had heard that . . ."

"That the heads of sexual collaborators were shaved and their breasts painted with a swastika? That was true." Simone stopped and pulled a package of cigarettes from her skirt pocket. I didn't know she smoked. She lit a cigarette and tossed the match onto a saucer with a practiced flip. Exhaling the first deep drag she shrugged and tossed her blonde hair. Then with her elbows on the table, holding the hand that grasped the cigarette, she leaned toward me, the cigarette smoke drifted before her narrowed eyes.

"What I did, I had to do. You can believe it or not." She sat back in the chair, her look daring me to disbelieve her claim. She greedily sucked on the cigarette again.

"Simone, I understand 'doing what you have to do.' You believe me."

"Somehow I think I do. Anyway I need to tell someone. I need some help from somewhere." She squashed her half smoked cigarette out in the saucer, lit another and began her account.

"In the beginning, my part . . . what I was supposed to do . . . was only to establish a contact within the German headquarters for the Resistance. You understand? Names, lists, gossip . . . that sort of thing. It was late in the war. You do not know . . . cannot begin to imagine what it was like for us. No food except what my parents grew in their garden. No heat, no electricity. It was like living in the shell of a city. All the conveniences . . . no . . . the necessities of life . . . just out of reach.

"And the humiliation. The hunger was agonizing, but the degradation was somehow worse. So when Denis made contact with me . . ."

I interrupted. "Denis! My Denis? Denis Denfert?"

"He was the leader of a Resistance cell. He is a Communist, you know. Very powerful."

No, I hadn't known. I'd have to ask Robert Sinclair what a *Communist* was.

Simone went on. "Anyway, Denis arranged for me to have a German government job. The Gestapo had their own secretaries, underlings, but these *assistants* had their own network of people who really did their work.

"I was employed by Max . . . well, his last name doesn't matter. He had to keep me well informed so I could perform accurate work for him to present as his own . . . and so you see how it worked. I passed on bits and pieces of information to Denis who used it . . . wherever it was appropriate, without deliberately betraying the original source. Max's group worked with logistics so the information mainly contained things like where supplies were stored or being transferred or transported."

"That was dangerous work, Simone."

"Not so much on an impersonal level. The war was nearing the end. Everyone knew that so there was much confusion and stupid commands and counter commands. No one was really in charge . . . would accept responsibility. It was easy for Denis and his workers to sabotage or steal supplies from the Germans without anyone realizing who had the ultimate responsibility.

"The worst part for me was when Max wanted to make me his mistress. It wasn't even out of affection or desire for me. It was to ensure my loyalty to him. To compromise me."

"Good Lord, what did you do." I coulda hit myself in the head for that question. I knew what she had done.

"When I told Denis what Max was suggesting . . . no, demanding, he wanted me to get out of the city. Go to the farm . . . anywhere away from Max. You see, *cherie*, I was a virgin and, by then Denis and I were in love."

Simone stopped here in her narrative and stood up and walked to the kitchen for an unopened bottle of wine and two glasses. She poured us a glass, taking a sip of hers, before she continued.

"The work I was doing was small but important in a starving city. All I know how to say here is that when I became Max's mistress, I was not a virgin. Denis and I . . . well, never mind. When the liberation began, I did escape to the country. My parents were dead by then. They had been caught up in another arm of the Resistance. It's ironic, they never knew what I was doing for our country and until their capture, I didn't know about their involvement either.

"Denis tried to help with their release, but by the time he located them, they had already been shot. He was unable to protect them like he did me when the war was over. That's why I have never had to bear the stigma of collaborator . . . why Michel and I have been free of the derision such women and their children have suffered."

"Why didn't you marry Denis?"

"When I knew I was pregnant with Michel, I lost my . . . oh, the word . . . the word . . . self-respect. Yes, that is it . . . self-respect. Max was not . . . *is* not a nice man, Bonita Faye. To regain my dignity, I needed to be independent. And who knows? Denis might not have ever been able to forget about Michel's father and after Michel was born, he and Claude were my only reasons for being.

"I did what I had to do," she repeated. "And it has worked, until now." Simone jumped up and started pacing the room.

"Why did you think Max was dead?"

"Denis told me Max died. Killed by a Resistance sniper during the liberation. Instead he was only badly injured and smuggled to Switzerland. That is where he has been since the war. Now he has slipped the border again and is here. And he wants Michel."

"No."

"Yes, I do not know how he found out he has a son. I've told you his injuries were severe. Max cannot father any more children. He wants Michel. He wants his only child.

"So . . ." Simone sat down and spread her red-tipped fingers in a helpless gesture on the table.

"You have to tell Denis," I said.

"Yes, possibly. I've thought of that, but I don't know if that is the best way. I hate to be dependent on any man to solve my problems. And, too, Max escaped from him once before."

"Right now, that's your best way . . . or . . ."

"Yes, what?"

"Let me think on it Simone. Let me think about it tonight. Don't worry, I'm not going to say anything about Max to Claude." Robert Sinclair was teaching me to think

before I leaped. Out of respect for him and in trying to
practice this new discipline, I held my tongue to keep
back the first answer I'd thought of besides telling Denis.
I'd almost said, let's kill the bastard ourselves. It's amazing how quick my thoughts went to the ultimate solution.

TWENTY

Ever since Patsy recited the Bible verse to me about the *"second death,"* I suspicioned I wasn't finished in the killing business. What really bothered me was how eagerly I accepted the challenge of killing Max. Maybe 'cause it had been so easy with Billy Roy. I liked planning things out ahead of time and Billy Roy's death had just happened naturally. Well, not naturally natural, but quick and easy. Figuring out how to kill Max would take some planning.

Simone had a message from Max the next day. It must have cut him to the quick to have to shelve his plans to take Michel, but someone from a former Resistance group had recognized him on the street and he had to sneak back across the border to safety. He'd phoned Simone from Switzerland.

"But he said he would be back as soon as he could. For me to be ready at any time to deliver Michel to him. And, if I told anyone about him, he would see that both Claude and I would be killed."

"Well, that really lets out telling Denis, but it buys us

some thinking time," I said. I wasn't ready to tell Simone my half-baked idea.

In the meantime, during our respite from the Max dilemma, I had taken to helping out at the hotel. Simone would accept hardly any money from me for my board and keep. She claimed it didn't seem right, but she did appreciate my now and then contributions that kept her from having to hire additional help. I knew I couldn't work for pay; I didn't have a French labor permit. In fact, I had already gotten an extension on my original visa, but like usual, I did what I could.

One of my Saturday chores was to polish the dark oak stairway with high smelling furniture polish. First I'd sweep away the loose dirt, starting from the top floor and then I'd get my bottle of greasy stuff and hand wipe with a cloth all the way down to the basement. The stairs were narrow and the work was easy even if I did come up shiny and gritty. I wore blue jeans and my head was tied up in a bandanna-like kerchief.

"Pew, you smell awful, Bonita Faye." Claude didn't like me to work on his Saturday day off even if that was the day he, too, helped around the hotel, lifting and moving furniture that was too heavy for Simone or the day maids.

He liked it better when I ran errands with him like delivering orders to the small business he and Simone ran from a house nearby. Two workers unpacked white demitasse cups and saucers and stamped them in pure gold with the image of the Eiffel Tower. Then they repacked the boxes and sent the cups to Paris to be sold in street kiosks as souvenirs to tourists. I still have one of those cups in my china cabinet in Poteau.

"Why is it always the Eiffel Tower?" I complained. "You French stick that tower on anything that doesn't move fast enough. Why don't you all try some different historic symbol, like . . . maybe, the guillotine?"

Claude wasn't any happier about my sending a weekly postcard to Harmon in Korea than he was about my being busy when he wanted to play. We were headed across the park in Boulogne to the Longchamp race track, when the problem finally came to a head.

I had begged him to let me stop long enough at the *Tabac* to pick up some more stamps—I never had enough stamps—when I noticed that he had gotten quiet ... too quiet. He'd been moody lately, but I hadn't thought that it had anything to do with me ... or Harmon.

"I read your note to Harmon Adams," he said.

"So? That's okay. I was just telling him about Robert Sinclair teaching me French." I thought he was worried about having read my mail.

"So? So who is Harmon Adams?"

We stopped in the middle of the path.

"I told you, Claude. Harmon is the deputy sheriff in LeFlore County who helped me out when ... when I needed help. He's my friend. Are you upset? You don't get upset when I write to Patsy."

"Harmon Adams is a man."

"That's right. A man who is the deputy sheriff of LeFlore County, Oklahoma. A man who helped me when my husband was killed. No, don't look away. You know I was married and that my husband was shot to death. Harmon is the man who made it easier for me to get through all that."

"And you care for him." It wasn't a question.

"Yes, I do. For lots of reasons. Maybe you do need to know some more about Harmon."

I spoke slowly so that he would understand what I was saying. Sometimes I struggled to substitute a French word for one he didn't know in English, but I told him Harmon's story.

About how Harmon had come from a poorer than dirt family in Oklahoma. How his pa was always drunk and beat up on Harmon and his mama and his little sister every time he'd had too much to drink. How Harmon used to steal chickens so they'd have something to eat. His ma had died giving birth to another baby and his sister had died of tuberculosis and his pa had shot himself.

"Harmon would have gone right on stealing all his life if he hadn't wound up in a foster home where the people were good to him. The man was a state trooper and the woman was a schoolteacher in Sallisaw. They gave him a second chance and Harmon paid them back by becoming a good man. They're both dead now, but he still lives by their rules."

Claude looked ashamed. "Do you think Harmon Adams would like me? I have not done much with my life."

"You're only getting started, Claude. Of course, you'll do something with your life. Be somebody. Anybody you want to be. And look what you've been through. A world war in your front yard, for goodness sakes. You don't have to do it all tomorrow."

His dark cloud lifted and he laughed. "Ah, but yes I do, Bonita Faye. Tomorrow is not soon enough. But, tell me one more thing." Claude pulled me close with one arm, close enough so that our bodies touched in every place. He ran the fingers of his free hand through my hair, then behind my head as he held my face close and kissed me. He asked me, "Does Harmon Adams love you as much as I do?"

There was no indication that the clouds scudding across the French sky were passing over sinister plots and life and death predicaments. Claude was wrapped up in some secret he wasn't telling and that was okay with me and Simone 'cause we were fooling around with our own.

"We cannot," she'd said in shock when I finally got up enough gumption to tell her what was on my mind.

"Cannot what?" asked Claude. Lord, we didn't know he was in the dining room, kneeling behind the service counter. "Sorry, I am repairing the plug to the hot plate," he'd added when he saw our shocked faces. "What is going between you? You look like I caught you stealing the wine." When we didn't answer, just continued to stare at him like dummies, he assumed a hurt and indignant pose. "I am going, I am going. Okay?"

"We cannot," Simone repeated in a whispered hiss when Claude left whistling. "We don't know how to kill someone. More than that, I don't know if I could kill another person."

"Not even to save your son?" I followed Claude, whistling his tune as I ran up the basement stairs.

Robert Sinclair knew me so well by now, that, he, too, was offended when I didn't share my secret with him. "What's going on with you, Bonita Faye. Why are you so mysterious all of a sudden? And, what's this sudden interest in Communists, the Gestapo, and the liberation? I thought you were more interested in 1789 than 1944." Puzzled, he scratched at the side of his receding hairline with the smooth stump of his left arm.

"And I thought you were teaching me about all of France's history," I replied in answer while I reached up to smooth his curly black hair into place. It was an affection gesture rather than a seductive tease. I gave his disorderly curls a final pat, like I'd seen Simone give Claude. "Now, you were telling me what you did in the war, about your part in the Resistance."

Distracted, he got caught up in his story again. "You've never seen anything like the devastation that was Paris when I arrived here. I came straight to the city after Normandy, one of the few who did, out a path through the lines, guided by a guerrilla fighter.

"The army's decision, the American army, that is, to head for the German border instead of liberating Paris at once was a difficult one for Eisenhower. On one hand, it would have been inspiring to the French and equally as demoralizing to the Germans to liberate the capital of France. A popular, sentimental, and symbolic demonstration of power. But, on the other hand, it was more prudent to conserve precious fuel for actual border fighting than to waste it on civilians in the city. Besides, we counted on the Resistance to continue to undermine the German authority here. I was sent in to do a reconnaissance of the situation in Paris. That's where I met Denis Denfert and Simone."

"You know Denis, too? And you knew Simone then? Why doesn't anybody ever tell me these things?"

"I guess we developed the habit during the war of not telling 'these things' and it's stayed with us. If you know about Denis and Simone, I gather you also know about their personal relationship?"

"That they were in love? Yes, Simone told me."

His voice thickened. "Did she tell you that I loved her, too?"

"No, she didn't. I didn't know, Professor."

Robert cleared his throat of whatever was making him choke and said, "Well, no matter, just another wartime romance, Bonita Faye. They were a dime a dozen back then. Now, what was it you wanted to know about land mines?"

"Oh, just if there were still any unexploded ones around?"

"You planning to blow someone up, Bonita Faye?" he joked.

Simone was grim-lipped and white-faced. "You have convinced me that it has to be done. That we have to kill Max. But, how?" We were walking in the Boulogne gardens, Michel skipping and tumbling ahead of us on the path. Simone never took her eyes off him and spoke only in English, although I had begun to help her son with some English words and phrases.

"Howdy do, ma'am," he said to one of the female statues along the walk. "I am hoping this is a good day for you." He strongly emphasized the "ing" in hoping. I wasn't going to make the same mistake with Michel as I had with Claude in the beginning. This kid was going to speak only the best English. "Cat got your tongue, you ol' thang?" He kicked the silent statue. Well, I never claimed to be no real schoolmarm.

Simone and I worked up a halfway decent plan, even scouted the site we had picked out for the murder; the Vermeillon's farm. Michel went with us and enjoyed the outing more than we did. As he ran between the rows of vegetables chasing butterflies, his mother and I drew up as accurate a diagram of the area as we could as we plotted the best way to kill Michel's father.

"Now, Professor, take a look at this. I want to know more about that gorilla fighting you're always going on about. Say if you was . . . were . . . going to come up on an enemy quiet like so as to gain the advantage of surprise? You followin' me? Pay attention now. Do you reckon the best place to hide is in this barn or behind this stone wall? And is a knife as good as a gun?"

"What are you up to, Bonita Faye?" Robert asked me for the fortieth time. "Where is this place?"

I answered him like always. "Why, I'm up to nothing, Robert. This is just a lil' ol' imaginary farm I drawed up to help me understand things." Then I made the mistake of adding, "I'm just that interested in what you, Denis, Simone, and Max did in the war."

"Max!" His good arm reached out and grabbed my shoulder. "Bonita Faye Burnett, what do you know about Max?"

Lord, God, it was easier to just pull out your shotgun and blow them away on an impulse than it was to figure out a complicated premeditated murder.

But when Max's call came through, Simone and I were ready.

I was at the bookstore, seated on my brown stool, my head bent over the map spread out on the counter, arguing with Robert like always. "I understand if you're hunched down in the barn, so the knife would come up under the ribs, but if I decide to hide behind the wall, I mean, if you were hiding behind the wall, wouldn't flat on the ground be better?"

I never did find out the answer to that one 'cause just then the door burst open with a bang as it hit the wall. Simone stood there wide-eyed and speechless. She could only nod her head toward me like a puppet.

"Heavens, Professor, I forgot I was going to help Simone with the marketing today. So, I'll just say bye now and mosey on with her." I took Simone's arm and led her outside. Talking for Robert's benefit I said, "What was it we were shoppin' for today, Simone? Beef or fish?"

Out of Robert's earshot, I asked her, "Did you tell Max where to meet you?"

She nodded and found enough voice to say, "Oh, *cherie*, he thinks I am going to have Michel with me."

"Good . . . good. That's the plan, Simone. Remember he's supposed to think that the farm is where you're going to deliver Michel to him. You gave us enough time to get there, didn't you?"

Again she nodded.

Shivering like someone had walked over my grave, I turned around to see Robert Sinclair standing with his right arm holding on to his bad one. I looked back again before we crossed the street to the hotel. He was gone, but I felt like I was still being watched.

It was a good day to be in the country. The sky was unusually clear and you could smell the hay that had just been cut. That upset me 'cause I was countin' on the tall grass to give us an additional advantage if we needed it.

Well, our first plan would just have to work.

Simone hid in the barn, hunched down just inside the darkened doorway, a butcher knife held in both her fists. Blade up. "You just stand up and push the knife in him.

Don't give Max time to talk. Just stand and shove. Can you do that, Simone?"

"Yes."

I wondered if she could. Maybe she wouldn't have to. Maybe I'd get him first. "When Max calls out, call him over this way. I'll be behind the wall along the way to the barn. It's going to be all right, Simone."

Sprawled in the dry grass behind the wall, I positioned my own kitchen knife and settled down to wait.

When Max drove the car into the farmyard, he parked it by the burned-out house. Even though the stone chimney and some foundation stones were all that remained, his natural instinct had been to park in front of what had been the main building. I had counted on that.

So far, so good.

Max got out of the car. I didn't look over the wall, but I could hear the sounds that told me he was shutting the car door. Then I heard him call, "Simone. Michel. Where are you?"

For a long minute, I didn't think Simone was going to answer, but in a weak voice, she finally yelled, "Over here, Max. In the barn."

He was coming my way. I could hear his feet on the gravel.

Just as I was getting ready to spring, Max surprised me. Three feet before he would have passed me, he jumped over the wall on my side.

I hadn't realized that my body was longer than the protection the wall gave it, and my sandals stuck out in clear view. Alert, Max had spotted my sprawled feet and jumped over to investigate. He didn't know who I was, but that advantage lasted only a second. He came straight for me, his hands outstretched. I jumped to my feet, thrusting the knife before me. His long arm reached over the knife and slapped me up the side of the head. Then he took the knife and turned it on me.

In French, he asked, "Who are you? Where is Simone? And Michel?" When he looked around for them, I charged him. The knife sliced into my upper arm and just as he raised it again, I heard a loud shot.

Max's head exploded in a red mass all over me.

From the barn, I heard Simone scream.

I stared down at the bloody bits on my shirt. There were squiggly white things mixed in with the blood. I looked down at Max who lay at my feet, face up. The front of his face was gone. Someone had shot him in the back of the head.

Just as everything seemed to go black, I saw two men jump over the wall. One held a rifle in both his hands. The other one only *had* one hand. It was Denis Denfert and Robert Sinclair.

Denis had shot Max. He had saved me from Patsy's lake of everlasting fire by committing my second murder for me.

TWENTY-ONE

We buried Max under the cauliflower. It was my decision. At first, I chose the green beans 'cause they had reached the end of their season, but I knew that if we put Max under the beans, I would never be able to eat them again, and I didn't like cauliflower to begin with. 'Sides those white things from Max's head reminded me of cauliflower which meant I'd never eat it again anyway. There was no sense in eliminating two vegetables from my diet.

Denis was the one who did all the work. Simone kept wandering around moaning and slinging her knife which Robert finally took from her, holding her close in a one-armed embrace. I was no help 'cause I was propped against the wall, trying to direct the operation, soaked from head to foot from when Robert had pushed me under the farm's old pump. I felt like the mess I looked. Rusty water ran down my face, plastering my hair to my head and, despite both our efforts, unsightly blotches stained my white shirt. Robert's handkerchief was tied around my upper left arm to staunch the blood from the wound Max had inflicted. It was a deep cut, but I didn't feel it.

132

There had been no tanks or air support, but the four of us were as shell-shocked as if we had survived a major battle.

Denis had the only shovel, but Robert found a hand rake in the trunk of Simone's borrowed car parked deep in the garage. He used it to scrape dirt and gravel over the blood Max had spilled at the murder site. It was already attracting flies. He also found a bottle of wine in the car.

We drank from the bottle.

"That cut will need stitches, Bonita Faye," said Robert.

"But that will hurt," I protested.

"For someone who doesn't like pain, you're certainly in the wrong business." His stubbed arm indicated the spot where Denis was dragging Max's body. We both watched as Denis tumped Max into his grave.

When enough dirt covered the dead man, we all relaxed. Denis stopped long enough to come over and take a turn at the bottle and give his own hug to Simone. He glared at me. "We'll talk about this later, Bonita Faye." I knew it. Denis Denfert spoke perfect English.

When we left the farm, it looked almost as undisturbed as it had when Simone and I had played there with Michel. Denis had carefully removed the remaining cauliflower heads before he began his digging and when he finished the burial, he moved them back in place. One good rain and nobody would ever know an ex-Gestapo officer lay under them. I wondered how many similar graves there were in France?

"Now we'll talk." Denis sat a fresh bottle of wine in front of us at the table in the Regina where we had all gathered.

My arm hurt and I was dizzy from the excitement, the pain and the wine. I had fainted twice during the stitching up at the infirmary where the attending physician . . .

a friend of Denis's . . . had not blinked an eye or asked one question about my injury. "Domestic accident" was what he had put on the medical report.

I tried to take control of the situation. "How did you know where we were? That Max was there?"

Denis actually sneered at me, his lip curling up on one side, but it was Robert who answered, "Bonita Faye, the next time you plan a combat maneuver, why don't you just run a flag up a pole with the target, time, and place on it? Your enemies wouldn't be surprised anyway and your allies would appreciate it."

Seeing my shamed face and maybe my pale condition, Robert softened his tone and continued, "Of course, I recognized the Vermeillon farm from your sketch, crude as it was. And your questions. From them I deduced that you had a killing in mind, but I didn't know who until Denis called me from Paris to report that Max had been sighted there. I remembered your mentioning Max to me.

"I contacted Denis again and told him what I suspected. He agreed with me that something was going on. But you were like a loose cannon. We didn't know which way you were going to shoot. He's been here in Boulogne ever since . . . waiting for something to happen."

That's why I had felt like I was being watched.

Robert went on, "When Simone burst into the bookstore, there was no mistaking the message she was conveying to you. Since we knew where you were going, I just had to locate Denis and get there as fast as we could."

Denis spoke of the event for the first time. "I am sorry Max cut you," he said to me. "I would have shot him sooner, but I was afraid I'd hit you." He ran his hand through his wiry hair. "I must be getting old."

"I'm glad you were there, Denis." I put my hand over his. "And you, Robert. I reckon I was kinda foolish, thinking Simone and I could pull it off by ourselves."

"No, no, Bonita Faye. Actually it was a good plan that almost worked. With a little more practice, you might have made it. I think you could have killed him," said Denis.

Simone still sat silent, but with the explanations and the murmur of normal conversation, the color that had begun to return to her face after she had hugged Michel on our return resumed its normal glow. Suddenly she sat bolt upright in her chair, "*Mon Dieu*, I just remembered."

"What?" we asked in unison.

"Max . . . the killing . . . the farm. We must never, never . . ."

". . . tell Claude." We finished the sentence for her.

We were laughing at this, our first laugh since the murder, when Claude himself strode into the room.

He dropped an armload of books on the table, upsetting glasses and spilling wine on the tablecloth. "So, it is over! *Fini!*"

"*Fini? Fini?* Claude, how can you know?" Simone rose from her chair.

"Because I have just taken my last examination. Because I am now a graduate of the University of Paris. That is how I know." For the first time, he stopped and looked around at us. "What is going on here? What has happened?"

Dear Harmon,

> *September is the same here as home. Turning cooler everyday. Claude has graduated from college. Simone and me are giving him a party at the Cafe Roy in Paris. Wish you were here to go to it. Nothing much else is happening. How are things on the 38th Parallel? Keep your head down and your gunpowder dry. Ha!*
>
> > *Love,*
> > *Bonita Faye*

P.S. this postcard picture is of the boats on the Seine where I have been many times.

Personally I thought everyone was always underesti-
mating Claude and his ability to understand. But then I
had the edge on Simone and the guys 'cause Claude and
me had a more intimate-like relationship. We told each
other everything. 'Cept I didn't tell him about Billy Roy
or Max and it turned out Claude was capable of keeping
secrets, too.

You'da thought we had signed a new treaty of Versailles the way everyone and their dogs carried on about
Uncle Martin letting me give the party at the Cafe Roy.
That was because of the menu I had selected. Fried
chicken, dog trot gravy over mashed potatoes and buttered corn-on-the-cob. Dessert was hot apple pie with
vanilla ice cream and good ol' American coffee. Bless her
sweet heart, Mrs. Blount had brought it to me from Har-
rod's gourmet food department in London.

Uncle Martin was a nervous wreck so I shooed him
on out of the kitchen, and his little chefs and I got along
just great. They thought the cream gravy was a white
sauce, but otherwise they just oohed and ahhed over
the aroma that filled the kitchen.

"Why you can walk down the street in Poteau every
Sunday at noon and smell this same food cooking in
every kitchen from First Street clear down to Main," I
said proudly.

Although it was a Sunday afternoon and the cafe was
open only for the party, that didn't stop passersby from
stopping and trying to order lunch. A group of American
tourists got downright huffy until they finally understood
it was a private party.

"Can we come back tomorrow and order the fried
chicken?" they asked as they left.

In addition to the pie, Simone had baked a big chocolate cake with one of them damned Eiffel Towers on it.
Claude's name was written around the bottom of the
tower in yellow icing and in honor of our shared tribute
to him, Simone had stuck a little paper American flag on
top.

"It was so thoughtful of you to bring the coffee," I said to Mrs. Blount as we enjoyed a cup at a little table away from all the relatives who gathered around Claude.

"I miss American coffee, too. Remember, I lived there for almost ten years. My husband went to America for the French government during the war and afterwards we just stayed on. When he died, I wanted to come home. To be with my family." She waved her hand, indicating the crowd.

"Don't tell me you're related to the Vermeillons, too?"

"But of course, *cherie.*"

But of course. How stupid of me to ask.

"Do not be surprised if Martin asks you to teach his chef how to prepare your fried chicken. I heard him telling my cousin that he is thinking of adding some American cuisine to his menu. Today has made quite an impression on our family, Bonita Faye." Inevitably she leaned forward.

I knew what was coming.

"And, tell me, little one, how are things, you know, between you and our Claude?"

I didn't have a chance to answer, because "our Claude" was coming our way with a package in his hands.

"Oh, another present. Who is it from, Claude?" I asked.

"From me. To you." He gave me the box.

"I don't understand. It's not my party."

"Oh, no. And the party is wonderful." And he bent down and kissed me on both cheeks in front of God and everybody. "This is a surprise. It has been ready for several days, but I thought today was the best time to give it to you. Open it, Bonita Faye."

I don't need to remind you that I don't like surprises. In fact, I can hardly be surprised, but Claude's gift just flat did me in. It was the first good surprise I'd ever had in my life and I keep a list of them.

Inside the box, under several layers of tissue was a handsome cream-colored mug. On it, in black enamel, was a modern outline of a French guillotine. The blade was a rich gold with a dash of bright red splashed across it. Vermilion red. In the center of the guillotine were the words *Liberté, Egalité, Fraternité*.

"Remember, this was your inspiration. I have double the orders for this cup than we had for the one with the Eiffel Tower. And I haven't even begun to show it around. Bonita Faye, with the extra profit, I can finance my first business venture. Already I have talked to several bankers who are interested in my ideas. As you say, my love, I am on my way to the clouds."

If I live to be a hundred, God willing and the creek don't rise, I will never forget the look in that young man's eyes that day as he stood there on the Champs-Elysees aholding on to that coffee mug. Those weren't clouds in his eyes, they were stars. If I could live my life over, the day Claude took his first step toward his dream would be one of the moments I would choose.

Claude had cups for everyone, the whole kit-and-caboodle of them. "It is the new Vermeillon crest," I heard him tell an old aunt as he pressed one in her hand. "From now on everyone will know us by this symbol."

I handed one of the cups full of hot coffee over Denis's shoulder and took the opportunity to whisper in his ear, "One thing more I don't understand. Why didn't you speak English to me that day you picked me up at the airport?"

Denis laughed and nodded for me to sit in the empty chair next to him. "You know I am a Communist? Yes? Well, maybe then you know we are becoming not so popular in America now?" Seeing the confused look on my face he said, "No matter. But you never know what kind of a conversation you're going to have with Americans. How many questions they will ask. It is more easier to not admit you speak the language."

"But it was just me," I protested.

"Ah, but then, *cherie*, I didn't know you were going to turn out to be *our* Bonita Faye."

TWENTY-TWO

The telegram was addressed to Mrs. Harmon Adams.

"What does this mean, this 'Mrs. Harmon Adams?'" Claude asked as he threw it at me.

"What does what mean?" I scrambled to pick up the envelope. "Oh, good Lord, I don't know. Should I open it?"

"No one else knows a Harmon Adams here, *monsieur* or *madame*."

"It probably has something to do with those insurance papers Harmon wrote me about," I said, but my heart was pounding as I tore open the telegram.

THE UNITED STATES ARMY REGRETS TO INFORM YOU THAT YOUR HUSBAND HARMON ADAMS HAS BEEN SERIOUSLY WOUNDED IN BATTLE. HE HAS BEEN AIR-EVAC'ED TO HAWAII FOR SURGERY AND CONVALESCENCE. LT. ADAMS HAS BEEN RECOMMENDED FOR A MEDAL OF HONOR FOR HIS ACTIONS AS WELL AS THE PURPLE HEART. THE UNITED STATES ARMY WILL KEEP YOU INFORMED ON THE CONDITION OF LT. ADAMS.

"Jesus Christ."

"Let me see it, Bonita Faye." He read the telegram.

"I gotta go home, Claude. No, I gotta go to . . . where did they say he is? Hawaii. I gotta go to Hawaii. Harmon needs me."

"No! You cannot go. The doctors will take care of him. I need you, Bonita Faye."

I saw Claude shouting and pleading, but his face seemed lopsided and his voice like an echo. My inner vision was seeing Harmon's dirty face when he walked into my living room one cold January night and said in a tired voice, heavy with an Oklahoma accent, "I love you, Bonita Faye."

"I love you, Bonita Faye." Now I could hear Claude clearly.

One real murder and one attempted one hadn't made me a woman. Nor the lovers I'd had. But right there in the lobby of the Hotel Regina . . . as surely as if a hand guided me over a bridge, I made a woman's decision. Only little girls think you can have your cake and eat it, too.

"And I love you, too, Claude. But Harmon loved me first. That's gotta count for something. I'm going to find Simone to help me make arrangements. We'll talk later."

Claude's shouts followed me all the way up the stairs. "Is it because he is older? A hero? Because he is from *Oklahoma?*"

I didn't have to look for Simone. She found me, sitting on the bed in my room, a half-filled suitcase beside me. "Where did I get so much stuff? I came over here with one little ol' suitcase and now look at all this. Pack rats don't have nothin' on me."

"Slow down, Bonita Faye." She sat beside me and took my hand. "Claude told me Harmon is injured. I understand your concern, but are you sure this is what you want to do?"

"I know it's what my insides are atelling me to do, Simone. Whether it's my heart, my soul or my guts speaking, I don't know, but something is telling me that if I don't go to him, that Harmon ain't going to make it. I couldn't live with that."

"What about Claude? I know my brother. He really does love you."

"And you gotta believe me when I tell you that I really do love him. More than I do Harmon in some ways, but that don't make it all the way right." I got up and walked to the open window. "Simone, I can't rightly put into words what this past year has meant to me. I came here more a wreck than you ever could imagine. I found acceptance of . . . well . . . me . . . from all of you, not just Claude. He's taught me how to love in a way . . . a gentle way . . . I've never known and Robert showed me how it's okay to be smart . . . and you and Denis have given me friendship and trust. I'm a new Bonita Faye, but I'll never know I'm the real Bonita Faye until I go back and see how I work out what I left."

Simone heard me, but she still continued to plead. "Michel loves you so, Bonita Faye. A year is a long time for a child. He thinks you've always been here and always will be."

"Now that's dirty pool, Simone. You know I couldn't love Michel any more than if I had borne him. I was going to kill for him. But, there's another child, a little girl, you don't know nothing about, that I owe somethin' too. Michel's got you and the whole Vermeillon clan to support him. I gotta find out who this little girl has on her side.

"Besides, Simone, I do love Harmon. Now are you going to help me get tickets out of here or not?"

She sat silent on the bed for a moment longer, her hands rearranging the clothes in my open suitcase. "You know, Bonita Faye, you are stronger than I am. I knew it at the farmhouse. You were so brave when Max attacked you, but even before that, the planning and the actual doing of it. Even if I had had the idea of killing

Max, I don't think I would have had the courage to carry it out."

When I started to protest, to remind her about her dangerous work in the Resistance, she stopped me. "And now. You are doing something else I can't do. You are making the decision between two men who love you and whom you love. I'll never be able to make a decision between Denis and Robert. That's what I admire and why I'll help you. Right or wrong, you have made a decision."

As we made reservations, bought more suitcases and even tried to telephone Hawaii, Claude ignored us. He simply refused to speak to me and Michel wasn't much better. He didn't understand why I was leaving him and hung on to his mother, crying behind her skirts.

Finally I took a long, last look at my Vincent van Gogh bedroom and, on impulse, jerked the framed postcard of the artist's own room from its nail over my bed. I was holding it as I followed Denis downstairs with the last of my baggage.

Robert was standing at the curb by the taxi. "I brought you some books for the trip." I hugged him. We'd already said our goodbye words. Then I hugged Simone. Michel and Claude had refused to come downstairs.

Just as I was stepping into the taxi, Claude burst through the door of the hotel. My gentle Claude, who had never touched me except in a loving way, grabbed my shoulders and shook me 'til my teeth rattled. Then he gave me a backbreaking embrace and kiss. The confrontation caused me to drop the framed picture, breaking the glass.

Claude didn't say a word, just turned and walked into the hotel, tears streaming down his face.

Robert picked up the postcard that had drifted apart from the frame during the fall and brushed it off. I held it in my hands as Denis drove us away from the Hotel Regina, leaving the shattered glass all over the sidewalk.

TWENTY-THREE

"Harmon Adams, how dare you** tell the United States Army that we're married and have them sending me next-of-kin stuff. Now you tell them the truth or you just get up out of that bed this minute and marry me. It's not right to lie to the United States Army." I ignored the tubes, the bags, and the wires and pulleys that surrounded the swaddled man I thought was Harmon.

His eyes were covered in bandages, but he smiled and said, "Goddamn, it's Bonita Faye."

They said he started getting better from that minute on. Hadn't I known that back in France? Sure as I'm standing here, I'll always believe that Harmon would have died if I hadn't gone to Hawaii to save him.

The next day, I stormed into the room again, talking while I tore off the mask the nurse said I had to wear. "Now, Harmon, listen up. If you don't marry me today, they're not going to let me come and see you. This here man I have with me is the chaplain of this hospital. He's Navy, but he'll have to do. Now all you got to say is yes, you are in your right mind and know what you're doin', and yes, you want to marry me, and he'll do it right here, right now. Is that clear?"

Harmon said, "Yes, I am, and yes, I do." Then he added, "Sir."

Who said real men don't cry? In less than a week, I had seen two of the strongest and most manly men I knew with tears running down their faces. Harmon's fell in little streams from underneath his bandages.

I don't like Hawaii. I don't care if that is where I got married. I can't even pronounce the name of the island the hospital was on and I resented the sun shining all the damn time. And the blue skies with their perfect cottonball clouds. I missed the gray skies of Paris with their fly-by clouds that let the direct sun in so seldom that it was no wonder that those Impressionist artists went bananas over light and shadow in their paintings.

"I don't like Hawaii," I told Harmon when I was pushing him in his wheelchair out onto the hospital's sun roof a few weeks after our bedside wedding. God knows, *sun* roof was a perfect name for it. "When can we go home, Harmon?"

"You talk to the doctors more than I do, Bonita Faye." His right leg was wrapped in shiny white plaster and stuck out in front of him. It didn't look comfortable atall, but I reckon it was a change from lying in bed.

"I ain't complainin', Harmon. I just want to get you home. Get those bandages off you and take care of you myself."

"I want the same, Bonita Faye. And I want to make love to my wife."

"Well, now, I reckon you are gettin' better if you're remembering what most newlyweds are supposed to be doin'."

"No sense in talking about it, if we can't do it. Now tell me some more about your Paris adventures. About the professor and the taxi driver. And Claude."

"Again? I think I wrote you every word I've told you these last few weeks. Didn't you ever read my postcards?"

"All forty-eleven hundred of them. And so did every G.I. in my outfit, not counting those at the mail depot in San Diego. Got so they would read them out loud before they'd hand them over to me. You got to learn to write letters, Bonita Faye. Strangers were coming up and asking me 'How's Bonita Faye? How many coffee cups has she sold now?' My own buddies were laying odds and taking actual bets as to whether you'd send me a 'Dear John postcard' that said you were marrying Claude."

"I hope the winner is buying beers in Korea," I said. " 'Sides I like postcards. You get in, say what you want, and you get on with it. A letter has too much space. And you get a picture, too."

"How come you didn't marry Claude? Didn't he ask you?"

"Harmon Adams, that's enough." I looked at the dark shadows under his tired eyes, the red, newly healed scar right above his temple and his yellow complexion. My heart hurt just looking at him.

The doctors told me to keep at him, to keep encouraging him and badgering him into getting well. "We've done all we can, Mrs. Adams. The rest is up to Lt. Adams and you. Right now, we know he'll live, but its a toss-up as to whether he'll be a cripple for the rest of his life. We can help him. We think he can make it, but we can't do it for him."

Harmon wouldn't get off his one-horse track. "Did you love him, Bonita Faye? Did you love Claude?"

I got down in his face. "I said that's enough, Harmon. Whether I loved Claude or not is my business and none of yours. If you keep up this whining about who it is I love, I'll walk off this pink oven of a rooftop and leave you to sit here until you melt or rot, whichever comes first. But, before I go, I'll tell you who it is I love. I love me. Bonita Faye Burnett Adams. And I only give myself what I want. And what I wanted was Harmon Adams. I flew across two oceans to get to him. And I married him. And nobody else. You got that straight, buster?"

Harmon sighed and smiled. "You really do love me, don't ya, Bonita Faye." It wasn't a question, but a statement of belief.

I settled back down in my chair. That was the last time Harmon ever whined and the last time he ever asked me about Claude.

We sat in silence and watched huge waves break way out in the ocean; the sunlight hitting the crashing water caused blinding rays of reflected light that gave me a headache. I said, "I hate Hawaii."

"I hate boats."

"Ships, you hate ships, Bonita Faye." Harmon leaned heavily on his crutches as he brought me another wet rag.

"Boats. Ships. It's all the same to me. The only good thing about it, is that it's taking us home."

"Now this isn't like you, to be so whining. You've got to shape up or ship out." Harmon's tone was warm and mocking as he wiped my forehead and mouth with the rag. "All I do is hear you complain. Let's see. You hate Hawaii. You hate ships." He grabbed ahold of the bunk to steady himself as the ship took a dip.

"Shut up. You're not funny. I hate you, too. Are we there yet? I knew we shoulda flown."

TWENTY-FOUR

"**B**onita Faye!" Patsy started crying the minute she opened the door and she couldn't do anything about the fluid that ran from her eyes and nose 'cause both arms were filled with babies, one braced against her hip and the other over her shoulder.

I took the smallest one. "Good Lord, Patsy, is this another one?"

"Yes, that's the new baby. He was born while you were in San Diego, but I didn't think there was time for Cherry to write you a note. And I didn't tell you I was expectin' 'cause Cherry don't know how to spell pregnant." Cherry was Patsy's oldest, the one who read my postcards to her mother, and the one who had sent me scrawled notes in France.

"What's this one's name? Terry?" Besides Cherry, Patsy had Harry, Jerry, Jr., Mary, Sary, and Carrie.

Patsy wiped her eyes and nose on the hem of her skirt. "It's Omega."

"Omega?"

"Yep, the last one. That's what I told Jerry and I don't want him to forget it."

We started laughing as only Patsy and I laugh. I hadn't forgotten the feeling. I just had kept it recessed somewhere when it hadn't been available to me. We finally had to set both babies and ourselves down on the floor to keep from dropping them.

I had on blue jeans and a T-shirt so I wound up wiping my eyes on the other side of Patsy's hem.

"God knows, I've missed you, Bonita Faye. I didn't think you were ever coming home again. After the first year, I began to think I'd just imagined you, and that Cherry and me were writing letters and getting postcards from somebody who didn't really exist." She reached out and pinched my cheek like she was proving I was real. She asked anxiously, "You ain't changed have you? You are still Bonita Faye, even if it is 'Adams' instead of 'Burnett'?"

"I'm the same all right."

"You look different."

"You haven't seen my hair this way before. And I've put on a little weight. Look, I've got real bosoms now." I cupped my hands over the T-shirt. We started laughing again.

"And Harmon? How is he, really?"

"Better. But, oh, Patsy, I know he's in such pain 'specially when he does his physical therapy. He went through a down spell in Hawaii, but his spirits have been the same ol' Harmon ever since. He's home now, in bed, waiting for me. I just came by to say *howdy* and to thank you for freshening up the house for us and for the food. I gotta get on back. Harmon might need something and he's gettin' so independent that he might stumble around and hurt himself. He's still not too steady on those crutches."

"And you're married to him. I declare. But, Bonita Faye, I wondered, but didn't get Cherry to write. Didn't want Harmon to read it . . . what about Claude? From your postcards, I figured you to be falling in love with him."

Everybody I knew wanted to know about Claude.

I hadn't heard a word from him in the four months since I'd left France.

Simone had written. And Denis. And Robert had sent books to Hawaii. He was determined to keep on with my education even if he had to do it long distance.

But only silence from Claude.

Every day Harmon and I walked the back country roads I loved so much. He switched from crutches to two and then one cane. He was really pushing himself. I liked amblin' so the slow pace didn't bother me none and we took advantage of those long walks to get to know each other again. He was glad I was reading different books and we'd talk about them, and gradual like I quit using the country English I'd started speaking again and began talking like Robert had taught me. If I had started out sounding different to Harmon, it would have scared him. He didn't want anything between us or about me to be different from what he had known before.

I asked silent forgiveness to Robert every time I said "ain't," but if one little illiterate word or a dropped "ing" now and then helped keep open the bridge between me and Harmon, it was worth it to backslide. The day Harmon corrected me was the day I knew he'd accepted a new Bonita Faye and I didn't have to play that role any more.

"Don't say 'ain't,' Bonita Faye. You're doing so well with your speech, you oughta try to stop saying words that aren't right."

"All right, Harmon."

Becoming lovers again took longer.

We had talked it over and agreed that to relieve

Harmon of any unnecessary stress, either mental or physical, that the initiative had to come from him. When he was ready . . . when he felt like it, I promised I'd be waiting. That didn't mean that as he improved that there weren't a lot of kissing and touching and holding. It was almost like being courted.

One afternoon after our walk, Harmon lay on our bed taking a nap. I tiptoed into the darkened room and placed some folded laundry on the bureau. As I was creeping out of the room, I glanced toward the bed. Harmon was watching me through heavy lidded eyes that weren't full of sleep. I recognized that look.

I walked toward the bed. "Are you sure, Harmon?"

"Will you help me, Bonita Faye?"

"Sure. Robert Sinclair says 'necessity is the mother of invention.' Let's see what we can invent."

Harmon's right hip had been shattered by the last burst of fire from the machine gun nest he'd charged. It was a mass of scars and the puckered tissue stood up in ridges against his thigh. The insides were held together with screws, nuts, and bolts. "And maybe a little bailing wire," he always joked.

He still couldn't bear much weight on it for long periods of time. So I got on top.

Afterwards, we cuddled together. "Maybe we didn't invent that way of having sex, but I bet I know where I could sell a lot of picture postcards of the way you looked while we were doing it."

"You hush, now." I snuggled closer and he absently stroked my arm.

"Where'd you get this scar? I don't remember it before." It was the thin line that Max had made on my upper arm.

"I had a 'domestic accident' with a kitchen knife," I answered as truthfully as I could. "And you're a fine one to be talking about my scars. You look as if you have the whole Battle of the Bulge mapped out on your hip. Aren't we a fine pair?"

"Yes, we are."

"We're really married now, Harmon, aren't we?"

"You goose, we've been married for five months."

"I know, but today, we're really married."

Leave it to Claude to know exactly the day Harmon and I consummated our marriage. I looked it up on the calendar in the kitchen when I got Simone's letter. Claude had married in Switzerland the same day Harmon and I first made love as husband and wife.

Her father was a banker in Geneva, one of the ones Claude had overheard calling him "a wonder boy." I remember Claude coming home to Boulogne and telling us about that after his first meeting with one of the financial cartels there. He'd never mentioned a daughter. She had a long, high-sounding name, but Simone wrote that everyone called her Didi. Claude always was the only one who could ever surprise me.

TWENTY-FIVE

Patsy's real Paris nightgown was red satin and had more black lace than my original one had. She strutted around her bedroom, throwing us into fits of laughter as she assumed what she thought was a model's pose.

"Bonita Faye, when Jerry sees this. . ."

"*Ooh, la, la,* Patsy. That's what he'll say."

"Well, he'd better be careful or I'll 'ooh' his 'la la.' "

When we'd stopped laughing again and Patsy was changing back into her housedress she told me, "Remember that little girl? That Elly Ross? From up toward Mountainburg? The one whose papa . . ."

"Yes, yes. I know who you mean. What about her?"

"My cousin Mary in Fayetteville sees her all the time. I told her to kinda take notes about what's going on and for to let us know how the kid's getting along. Is that okay?"

We stared at each other over the discarded gown and stack of presents on the bed between us. I was slow to answer. "Yes, I think that will be just fine, Patsy. Do you think Mary would like one of those silk scarves from Paris? Just as a little 'happy'?"

"I think one of the red ones."

"Yes, a red one."

Settling back into Poteau, Oklahoma, was a definite culture shock. It might of been extra maturity on my part, but I saw the people different. Each one took on a depth of character I hadn't noticed before. When I recognized them, that is. I was only gone less than two years, but when I ran into someone at the market or the gas station, they'd just go on and on about how they had missed me and how good I was looking and how was Harmon?

I'd answer and say all the right words, but most of the time I didn't have any idea in the world who it was I was talking to until about an hour later. Then it would hit me like a ton of bricks. "Well, I'll be. That was Mrs. Pearleman . . . or . . . Old Lady Shaw" . . . and so on.

It didn't matter. No one in all of Oklahoma, except Patsy, of course, wanted to know about my time in France. No one wanted to look at my pictures, hear me speak French, or even ask how the weather was in France. Finally I got where when they'd say, "Now where was it you've been at, Bonita Faye? New York City?" I'd answer back, "Why, I've just been away at school."

You're not going to believe that I didn't recognize Miss Dorothy, but it wasn't all my own fault. She'd started bleaching her hair yellow. 'Cept it had a greenish cast to it.

"Bonita Faye Burnett. Oh, I am sorry. It's Adams now, isn't it?"

Most of the time when I didn't know somebody who knew me I'd just smile and fake it. Most people want to talk and tell you about themselves anyway and don't care about anything 'cept if you're listening. So I'd just nod whenever it seemed appropriate and they'd be satisfied. But I just stared at this woman. I had never seen her before in my life.

"It's me. Dorothy. Over to the post office?"

"Oh, yes. You look different somehow."

"Just keeping up with the times, honey. I just wanted to tell you that I read all the postcards you sent everybody. Hope you don't mind, but it gets so boring around here and you were having such an exciting time. Poteau must seem dull to you now. How's your friend Claude? Did he get that job in Switzerland that you wrote Patsy about? You know, I always thought something was going on b'tween you two. Just goes to show you how wrong a body can be. You married to Harmon now and all."

Later, the more I thought about Miss Dorothy, the madder I got. The nerve of that bitch. Her and her green hair and day-glow yellow dress. I hadn't cared when she'd slept with my first husband, but reading my United States of America mail was another matter. Why, that was against the law. That's when I got the idea to do what was probably the only truly mean thing I've ever done in my life.

The next time Harmon and me went to Fort Smith, I picked up a postcard of Judge Parker's courthouse and sent it to Miss Dorothy. I wrote it with my left hand while I was in the bathroom of the courthouse and mailed it from Fort Smith before we left.

Dear Dorothy,

I just had to write and tell you how pretty you look in that new yellow dress of yours. You should always wear that color. It goes so good with your pretty hair. We can never meet, but I will always be

Your Secret Admirer

For the rest of her life, you could see Miss Dorothy coming a mile away. She never wore anything but that god awful shade of yellow and she always kept a yellow-green bleach on her hair.

And I took to putting my postcards in sealed envelopes.

Six months after I left Paris, three months after Harmon and I came home to Poteau, I had a letter from Claude. It was written on cream-colored, heavy paper with a black-engraved guillotine splashed with Vermeillon red up in the left hand corner. It was just like the cups, but the words *Liberté, Egalité, Fraternité* were missing and the name of Claude's company had been added.

Dear Bonita Faye,

The souvenir cup line continues to thrive. Since you were the one who had the original idea of designing, packaging, and marketing our first successful product, it is my pleasure to inform you that Vermeillon, Ltd. has been putting aside 50% of the profits of the venture for you. It has now reached a considerable sum. Please notify my solicitors as to where you would like the money deposited.

Sincerely,
Claude Vermeillon

I sent him back a postcard of the gallows in Fort Smith that said, "50% is too much. Will not accept."

Three weeks later I got another letter with just the number "40%" on it.

I wrote back on a postcard of fall in the Ozarks. "10%."

The return offer was "30%."

My answer on a postcard of the Tahlequah Trail of Tears was "15%."

The return reply of "20%" was written on a postcard of the Eiffel Tower.

"Done. Send it to First American in Poteau, Oklahoma." I sent it on a postcard of an Arkansas Razorback Hog.

It wasn't much in the way of communications, but as my friend, Robert Sinclair, had taught me, communications between two people start simple and build. Claude and I had done it before when we didn't even speak the same language. I didn't see why we couldn't do it again. The only difference was that this time we were speaking in numbers instead of French. It was all the same to me; just another foreign language.

I was right in that I didn't think Harmon would use the money from France. He said, "We don't need anything from Claude."

"The money's not Claude's, it's mine. I earned it."

And I had, too. In the months following Claude's graduation party, I had taken to the roads with that damned coffee cup. It was bigger than the French vendors were used to selling, so I upped the price on it. They kept saying that bigger wasn't necessarily better, but the ones I did sell to kept calling me back for more. Seems the American tourists preferred it over the smaller ones.

I had to be the salesman 'cause Claude was taking off like a ball of fire in the financial world and was gone all the time, so it was Denis Denfert who would drive me to a broker's office where Claude had set up a meeting. The "howdys" went okay, but when we got down to business, inevitably I'd have to say, *"Doucement, s'il vous plait,"* but they'd start speaking louder instead of slower. So I'd go out to the taxi and drag Denis in, and he would interpret for us. We'd wind up smiling and shaking hands with one and go on to the next name on Claude's list. Denis and I became quite a sales team.

Friday nights when Claude came back to Boulogne from wherever he had been during the week, usually Switzerland, I'd try to show him the orders and the business of the week. All he wanted to do was hold me close and love me, so I just learned to wait until Saturday morning. I knew there was a lot of money coming in, but I also knew that it took a lot of money to finance Claude's debut into the business world. It never occurred to me then that any of the cup money was mine.

Claude couldn't afford to give me any of it when I was in France, but he musta kept a record of the profits and now that he was doing so well, he wanted to do the right thing. Well, I'd earned it, so I'd take it and say "thank you very much." Only when they called me to the bank to sign a receipt and to have some contracts Claude had sent over notarized, I was shocked at the large amount my 20% represented. For one brief greedy second, I thought, Jesus Christ, I could have had 30% more.

John Falkenberry was the banker and he fawned all over me. At first I thought it was 'cause it was such a lot of money, but actually it was because he was a dirty old man. I didn't give him the time of day, and, in fact, thought about moving my money to Fort Smith, but then I thought, what the hell, I'd forget those rumors of why he supposedly had to leave his last job. Let bygones, be bygones. And I let him have the money . . . for one month. Then I couldn't stand it, I switched, not only the money from France, but also our main account to the City National Bank in Fort Smith. I felt a lot more secure after that. In case you think I'm paranoid about money, you might remember that I first knew John Falkenberry by another name. Billy Roy and I used to call him "Judge."

Harmon eventually let me spend some of the money on our visit to Washington, D.C., when he finally felt like making the trip to receive the Congressional Medal of Honor. He wanted to stand on his own two feet when he shook hands with the President of the United States of America.

* * *

When we got back to Poteau and were taking one of our daily walks and discussing our future plans, was when Harmon told me he didn't ever want to kill anybody no more. With one successful and one unsuccessful death notched in my belt, I knew how he felt. I didn't want to plan any more killings in my lifetime either.

"What would you think if I went back to college?" he asked.

"Why, I think that'd be just fine, Harmon. What are you aiming to be?"

"Anything. As long as I don't have to wear a gun to work."

TWENTY-SIX

Stillwater, Oklahoma, is more of a foreign country than France ever thought about being. I look back on our time there as being strictly in limbo. We went to classes. We ate. We studied. We made love and we slept in our stupid little apartment where I had one dumb geranium that never bloomed 'cause I watered it too much. I didn't realize Harmon hated it there as much as I did until he came home one day and said, "The LeFlore County Commissioners want me to run for sheriff. What do you think?"

"I thought you didn't ever want to have a job where you had to wear a gun again?"

"Well, I've been thinking it over. A sheriff runs things from the sheriff's office. He doesn't have to go out and corral criminals. He just has to see that it's done." He asked again, "What do you think?"

"Sounds to me like you've already made up your mind, Harmon."

"Yeah, I reckon I have. Let's go home, Bonita Faye. The campaign kick-off luncheon is this Tuesday."

I threw the geranium out the window and packed our bags.

Since nobody in their right mind would run against a two-time, genuine hero, Harmon won the election by a higher percentage than had ever been recorded in LeFlore County. He was back in a brown uniform and I was back in one of the only two places where I liked living: Poteau, Oklahoma.

Robert Sinclair came to visit us in Poteau the first Thanksgiving Harmon was sheriff. He'd come back to the States to say his goodbyes to his sick mother in Pennsylvania and after she died, he dropped down to Oklahoma. I don't need to tell you how glad I was to see him.

"I am so pleased that you've continued your studies, Bonita Faye." I wondered if Robert knew that after so many years in France that he talked English with a French accent? "Tell me about your classes and your grades."

"Oh, I didn't get any grades, Robert."

"Bonita Faye, how could you go to college and not get grades?"

"I just picked out classes that interested me and audited them. You don't get grades for auditing."

"You weren't registered? I don't understand."

"Robert, you don't think I was going to tell those people in Stillwater that I had never graduated from high school, do you? I'd of died of shame. Besides I graded myself."

"And what did you make?"

"An A in all the English courses. And in the literature classes. A B in psychology and biology. I didn't pass math, but squeaked by science."

"And did you take, I mean *audit*, the French class like I told you to?"

"Yeah, but they don't speak French in Stillwater like they do in Paris. I gave the teacher an F."

"That's my Bonita Faye." He laughed and added, "But maybe the teacher didn't have to learn perfect French or starve to death in a cafe on the sidewalks of Paris."

Robert and Harmon hit it right off. Harmon even seemed more relaxed and easy about my time in France when Robert was there.

He said, "Robert Sinclair is a hell of a man. Wish I had known you had such good people looking out for you over there. I wouldn't have worried so about you."

That was probably the maddest I ever got at Harmon Adams.

Robert brought me up to date on all the goings on in Paris and Boulogne. "Denis and I still keep trying to force a decision out of Simone. We've told her time and again, choose one or the other, but just choose. She says she can't do it . . . that she loves us both too much.

"The funniest thing is that Denis has become a capitalist. As you know, after you left, Claude hired him to run the souvenir end of the business. As you would say, he took to it like a fish takes to water. Gave up his taxi and wears a suit and tie every day. He even moved into the Regina."

"But, Robert, doesn't that give him an advantage with Simone?"

He grinned. "No. I gave up my flat and moved in there, too."

Even in America we call that a *ménage à trois*.

I didn't like what he had to say about Michel.

"Simone hates to admit it, but the boy's troubled. We think someone has told him that his real father was German. That's still a big deal in France. Anyway, something has changed him. He's not happy and he gets into trouble more than a boy his age should. We're all worried about him."

We talked awhile about Michel and then I asked Robert the question I had been putting off. "And Claude?"

Robert's face lit up. "I guess it's because I'm sitting here in Oklahoma that your phrases leap to my mind, but

Claude is no 'flash in the pan.' His reputation for business acumen continues to grow. To be as young as he is, he is certainly a successful man. And you should see him with his daughter. Didi swears she'll be spoiled beyond redemption by the time she's grown."

"You mean little Franchesca? Claude and Didi sent me an announcement when she was born."

"Yes, but Claude started calling her *Belle*. Now we all do." Always the teacher, Robert continued to explain. "That's French for pretty like your name *Bonita* is Spanish for . . ." He stopped. "So that's why Claude . . ." Robert was embarrassed.

"What's the matter, Robert? Do you think you and Denis and Simone have cornered the market on love triangles?"

"Sarcasm doesn't become you, Bonita Faye. That wasn't fair."

"No? Well, I've learned that the only fair in this world is the one where they give out blue ribbons to prize hogs." I quit it. I wasn't being fair. "I'm sorry, Robert. It's just that Claude and I parted so suddenly. And with such drama." I threw up my hands and laughed. "I know that's the French way, but we left so much unresolved."

"It's been three years, Bonita Faye. Don't you think it's about time you left Claude?"

"But I did."

"I meant emotionally."

I was some surprised when I heard Harmon tell Robert that we'd be over to France to visit him. "It would mean a lot to Bonita Faye to see her friends again. We'll make the trip just as soon as I can wrangle the time away from the office."

After Robert left, I took my troubles over to Patsy. I sat at her kitchen table holding Omega while she ladled but-

ter onto thick homemade bread slices that she then
sprinkled with sugar. The slabs of bread and a pitcher of
strawberry Kool-Aid were passed out the back door to
Cherry to distribute for an afternoon snack for the kids.

"Patsy, I count more than six kids out there. Did you
have another one while I wasn't looking?"

She handed Omega a slice of the sweetened bread and
stuffed some in her own mouth. "Nope, them's the neighbors' kids. Always seem to know when there's food
floatin' around. I always make extra." She reached over
and patted Omega on his round head and said again,
"Nope, like I told you Omega is the last of the bunch.
And, is he spoiled."

"That reminds me what Robert said about Claude's
daughter."

"Is that what's eatin' you, Bonita Faye. Claude? You
want to talk about it?"

"Patsy, what does it say in your Bible about somebody
loving two people at the same time?" I knew Patsy would
rather have her tongue cut out than ever gossip about
our conversations.

"Well, let me think. You know in the ten command-
ments, it says that about not coveting your neighbor's
wife?"

I nodded.

"But, that commandment is for a man. I'm not that
sure about women. Then there's that part about *whither
thou goest*, but that's really a woman to her mother-in-
law. And an ex-mother-in-law at that. Can you imagine
anyone being that crazy about a mother-in-law? And, I
know you have to marry your dead brother's wife, but,
Claude and Harmon aren't brothers. 'Cept maybe in the
biblical sense. But that don't even count 'cause one of
them ain't dead."

She paused and ate some more sugared bread. "I'm
stumped, Bonita Faye. Seems like all them rules are
made for men. Let me get my Bible." I waited while she
got up and found the big white family Bible that I had

given her when I found out she'd learned to read. Cherry had taught Patsy when the first grader had started school. They'd learned together. I knew she was using getting the Bible as an excuse to think 'cause there weren't words written in that book that Patsy didn't know by heart.

She brought it back and sat it on the table, but didn't open it. With one hand on the Bible, she said, "Now Paul had a lot to say about women and most of it not worth spit. That man didn't like women, Bonita Faye. I swear, I can't think of a single case of a love triangle in the Bible. Oh, no, that's not the truth. There was David and Bathsheba. But David was the one who settled that one, too.

"Bonita Faye, is this here triangle between you and Claude and Didi? Or Harmon and Claude and you? A triangle has three pointy corners, don't it? Sounds to me like we've got us a square here. Maybe that's why nothin' comes to my mind. I don't know nothin' about no 'squares' in the Bible."

"Sometimes, Patsy, I think it's just all in my imagination."

Two more years passed before Harmon and I made the trip to France. You can do a lot of thinking in two years.

TWENTY-SEVEN

I have always enjoyed flying and I can't abide those women who squench up their eyes and shake their hands and say, "Ooh, ooh, I don't think I could ever get on a plane, ooh, ooh." Makes me sick to hear them.

You'd think I wouldn't like flying 'cause the person in the passenger end doesn't have any control and you know how I like to be in control of situations at all time. However, maybe that's just why I *do* like flying. It's one of the few times in my life that I don't have to be the driver.

A funny image always comes to my mind when I fly or when I'm working in my garden at home and look up and see a jet stream overhead. There'd go the plane, and I'd be sitting there planting petunias thinking of the Wonder Woman comic book pictures of Wonder Woman sitting at the controls of her invisible flying machine. Always thought if I could see through to the insides of an overhead plane, I'd see people sitting and walking on air. Or reading, eating, and visiting the john up there in the clouds and all the while they'd be hurtling hundreds of miles across the earth.

When I was flying, I wondered if anyone was looking up at me.

In March of 1957, I received a telegram from Simone.

PLEASE COME AT ONCE. MICHEL AND I NEED YOU AGAIN.

"You can go with me or not, but I'm going."
"Don't get your dander up, Bonita Faye. I'm going."

Harmon and I landed at the Paris airport shortly before noon on a Tuesday early in April. Simone, Denis, and Robert were there to meet us when we finally filed through customs.

"Where's Michel?" was the first thing I asked. Where's Claude was what I was also thinking.

"Claude and Didi are waiting at the Regina with Michel and their children. Michel doesn't have the cast off yet and, well, we didn't want to frighten Harmon by acting too much like a gypsy reunion at the airport," said Simone.

Just like with Patsy, there were no barriers to recross with Simone. I don't know if it is just my style or what, but once I call a person friend, they are always my friend, right or wrong. Simone hugged me and held me at arms length to admire my dress, travelworn as it was. I had already told Harmon I'd hit him up the side of the head if he told anybody that I had spent two days in Dallas at Neiman Marcus, buying a wardrobe to wear to Paris. I wasn't in competition with Didi, but I wasn't going to let her put me in the shade either.

When I exclaimed that I didn't know Michel was in a cast and how bad was he hurt, and how was he hurt, Simone hushed me and said, "Later, *cherie.*"

Denis drove us to Boulogne in the big black car he'd traded the taxi in for. I kept sneaking peeks at him from over the back seat to make sure that this distinguished, dark-suited man was really my Denis Denfert. Denis spoke English to Harmon and we all had a laugh, at my expense, I might add, about the first time Denis had picked me up outside an airport.

Robert and Harmon picked up on their friendship where it had left off just like me and Simone, but I knew my Harmon well enough to know that he was nervous about meeting Claude. One of the ways I could tell was how he kept brushing back his short brown hair with his hand until finally it was all just one big cowlick. He seemed more comfortable when we finally arrived at the Hotel Regina and could see that it wasn't a fancy place where he would feel awkward and self-conscious. I had told him so, but you know Harmon, he always had to see for himself.

There wasn't anyone in the lobby to greet us either, so it was after Denis and Harmon had taken our bags up to a second floor suite where we'd freshened up a bit and after we'd descended into the basement dining room before we saw the rest of the family.

It was Michel, sitting in a wheelchair with a plastered leg raised on a lift, who first captured my attention. He was a sturdy boy of eleven with blonde, cowlicked hair like Harmon's, but his invalid state made him look small, helpless, and afraid. His blue eyes had dark circles under them and his normally ruddy complexion was pale. My heart went out to him and I sank to my knees by his chair.

"Michel. Oh, Michel. I've missed you so much. Do you remember me? Do you remember your Bonita Faye?" I spoke in French.

His answer was to put two young arms around my neck and hold me in a tight embrace. Our tears mingled and once again I tasted the salty skin of the little boy I used to know so well.

I looked up and, with my carefully applied mascara running down my face, I saw the other boy I had left behind. A handsome dark-faced, slender man with moist eyes who held out his hands and helped me to my feet and kissed me on both cheeks in the French way. "Welcome home, Bonita Faye," Claude said.

Then I watched as the hand that had gripped my shoulder during the brief embrace extended to grasp that of my husband.

"Claude Vermeillon. Welcome to France."

"Harmon Adams. Pleased to be here."

They stood staring at one another and I was taken by the similarity of the color of their eyes. Both sets of eyes were a rich brown, but I knew if I ever found myself in a room with just one each of their eyeballs, I'd know which was Claude's and which was Harmon's.

Then Claude turned and introduced his wife. "Bonita Faye and Harmon Adams, I would like you to meet my wife, Didi."

We shook hands and smiled, and when we did, it seemed like everyone in the room started to breathe and talk at the same time—like their held-up breath just had to make words when it was expelled.

Didi Vermeillon was everything I thought she would be and everything I was not. She was tall, maybe even taller than Claude, with a clear, rich complexion and green eyes. Her long blonde hair was swept up in a smooth French roll with one perfectly placed, perfectly splendid curl left loose at the end of the roll so that it could hug her long white neck. She was dressed in a simple cream-colored silk dress that emphasized her flawless figure and she smiled at me with even white teeth through naturally red lips.

I liked her. Didi was exactly the woman I would have chosen for Claude myself if he had asked me to go wife-shopping for him. And Didi liked me.

Why we were just one big happy family.

We played with Claude's perfect little children, four-year-old Franchesca, oops, *Belle*, and tiny year-old Francois. We made much ado over them and Michel. And we ate a lot and we drank gallons of wine. Both red and white. If it hadn't been for the inconvenience of jet lag, I think we'd be there still, but suddenly I found myself in our bedroom, throwing up in the commode. I was glad we were in one of the few rooms in the Regina that boasted an attached bathroom.

There were no flowers on my pillow, but a big bouquet of multi-colored roses stood on my dressing table. I bet Didi arranged every one of them her own self.

We slept late the next morning and, in fact, I slipped out of bed, dressed, and went downstairs, leaving Harmon snoring away. Simone was in the lobby and after giving a few instructions to the desk clerk, she followed me on down to the dining room.

"Sit down, Bonita Faye. I'll serve you your coffee. Do not worry, I remember exactly how you like it."

After my second cup, I leaned forward and said, "Okay, Simone. What is it? What's going on here? Who hurt Michel? Do we have to kill someone?" I was only half joking.

Simone's story confirmed to me what Robert had suspected two years ago. Someone from the old Resistance group had gossiped about Michel's real father and as that sort of thing usually goes, it became common knowledge in several households where some children had overheard their parents' conversations. The children, being children, eventually repeated the harmful rumors on the playground and began to taunt Michel.

"Michel never told me. Never asked me any questions. He just wore down under the insults and finally fought back. Several boys ganged up on him and pushed him off a wall in the park. It was a bad break, but it has healed. The cast comes off next week, but after the first shock of the injury, he cried continuously for days. Then, and this was worse, he just sat in bed or the wheelchair expressing no emotion at all. And he refuses to talk to me about . . . Max." I noticed furrowed lines in Simone's forehead, the kind you get when you frown too much.

"What about Denis or Robert?" I asked.

"They have both tried to explain to him. You know . . . what it was like during the war. How everything was a matter of life or death. Denis even volunteered to say he was Michel's father, but it's too late for that." Simone reached a hand out to cover mine. "*Cherie*, it was probably too much to ask, but I remembered how you helped us before. You're so good with ideas, I thought maybe . . ."

"Does Claude suspect what this is all about?"

"That is another strange tale, Bonita Faye. Claude has known all along. He never let on because he knew I didn't want him to know . . . out of respect for my feelings. He has tried to talk to Michel also, but the child will not listen to anyone. Oh, what are we going to do?"

Five years before I had sat at that very table planning how to take a life. Now I was being asked to help save one.

"Let me think on it, Simone. We'll come up with something."

I don't know which I enjoyed more—showing Paris to Harmon or watching Paris react to my husband. Harmon was a beautiful sight, walking down the Champs-Elysees with his blue jeans, brown leather jacket, western hat, and cowboy boots. More than one Parisian asked him if he was John Wayne.

If I thought he was getting too cocky about it, I'd walk away and hide around a corner, leaving him to try to talk to his admirers. In just a few minutes, he'd bellow out, "Bonita Faye, come on back here and help me out of this."

We toured the Louvre and I showed him my lovely Winged Victory and my favorite Impressionists' paintings. And the Mona Lisa. "You can't come to Paris, Harmon, and not see the Mona Lisa."

We went up in the Eiffel Tower and rode the boats on the Seine. And I even got him to a play at the Theatre of Paris. It was our first vacation ever and while he en-

joyed the adventure of it I could tell he was happiest on
the days we stayed in Boulogne and he walked down to
Robert's bookstore to jaw awhile or when he sat and
drank coffee with Simone.

"I finally understand why you left France. Even why
you left Claude. Your Harmon is quite a man," Simone
said. Everyone liked Harmon and even Michel began to
talk to him. He was in awe of this big "cowboy" from Oklahoma, but wasn't at all shy at practicing his English
with him. Robert had kept up Michel's English lessons
all these years and although he spoke with an accent, his
vocabulary was astonishing.

I watched the two of them sit together in a little outside patio that was new to me at the Regina. Simone
said it was only for family, that it helped them get away
from the continual openness of the hotel. The patio door
was halved . . . a Dutch door Simone called it . . . and
when I stood just inside it, and the top half was opened
outward, I could see the patio visitors without them
noticing me.

Harmon was telling Michel about Oklahoma. He'd die
before he'd let anyone back home go on about his famous shoot-out in Panama, but now I heard him tell the
wide-eyed youngster about the cold and rainy January
night he'd shot four desperadoes. And how about he, too,
had once walked with crutches.

Harmon was raising up his shirttail to show Michel his
scars when Simone came up behind me and slipped an
arm around my waist. We watched the two in the garden
and exchanged an understanding look. I nodded in answer to her unasked question.

TWENTY-EIGHT

*C*laude dropped a pink rose in my lap. *"Bonjour, Madame,"* he said as he sank onto the wrought iron bench next to mine.

"Bonjour, Monsieur Vermeillon." I dropped the letters I had been reading and picked up the rose. "This is a surprise. I thought I wouldn't see you again until we visited you in Geneva."

"I had a little business in Paris, and it is not so far to Boulogne from there, so . . ." he shrugged as only the French can.

"Harmon is at Robert's," I said like the dutiful wife I was. "He'll be sorry to miss you. Can you stay for supper?"

"Yes, I know where he is. Simone told me. She also told me that you were here at the park. It is you I wanted to see."

It had been five years since Claude and I had been alone together. During the "family" reunion we had spoken, but mostly about our mutual business dealings. Neither of us had exchanged looks that signified anything other than an honest delight at seeing one another again.

"I think there are some things we should say, Bonita Faye."

"Yes, Claude."

"And now is the time."

"Yes, Claude."

Silence.

"Well, what are they?" I asked.

"Give me time."

"You've had five years."

We laughed in the old way and with the release of laughter, we found the plane we had been seeking.

In a more comfortable way Claude said, "I was hurt when you left me."

He paused to look at me and when I didn't answer, he went on. "Now that I am older . . . *mon dieu* . . . I was young then . . . I understand more about what happened between us. I thought it was for always. . . ." He stopped. "I have worked out a lot of it in my mind, but there is one question I have always wanted to ask you."

"Yes?"

"If Harmon had not been injured . . . if there had not been the threat of his dying . . . would you have stayed with me?"

I'd had the same years to think of an answer to that one. Without hesitancy I answered, "Yes."

A satisfied smile crossed his lips. "Have you ever regretted going?"

"No." And that was the truth. Over the years I'd spent wondering and playing "what ifs" in my mind, my going to Harmon in Hawaii and marrying him there was one thing I'd never regretted.

"I love Harmon, Claude."

"I have always known that."

"And I love you."

"*Aie!*" he groaned. "That is not fair."

"The County Fair."

"What does that mean?"

"It's a saying back home. The only fair is the County Fair. Let me ask you something. Do you love Didi?"

"But of course, but that is . . . No, it is not different. I could not imagine my life without Didi." Claude took my hand. "Are we always going to love each other, Bonita Faye?"

"I hope so, Claude."

There. We had said most of the words I had imagined in my head for ages. And we were still friends and lovers. Oh, not in a passionate sense, but in the feeling anyone gets when they know another loves them. I've always thought there was too little of that in life. Too few people who said they loved you when they did.

We stood up and I took Claude's arm and we walked through the park together.

"What really is not fair is Simone, Robert, and Denis," Claude said.

"I understand what you mean, but it seems all right for them. I couldn't live that way. I'd have to make a decision."

Claude threw back his head and laughed. "Well, we all know that." Then seriously he asked me, "Why do think Simone is not able to do so? To make a decision?"

"Well, now that I know that you know all about her work in the Resistance and about Max . . ."

"Yes, I know. Michel's father."

"Well, I think it's all tied up in that time. Or maybe it has something to do with our killing Max. . . ."

Claude stopped in the middle of the path and grabbed my arms. My letters and the rose fell to the ground. "Killing Max! Max is dead? Who killed Max?"

It was hard to answer with him shaking my arms, but I said, "Claude, I thought you knew. Simone said you knew all about Max so I thought you knew she and I killed him. Well, not really, it was Denis. And Robert, too, of course . . ."

"Denis? And Robert? You and Simone? When?" He kept on shaking me.

"Let me go. It was when you graduated from the university."

He didn't let go. "Where? How?"

In between the shakes that were making my head hurt, I tried to tell Claude how it had been. Most of it came out as hiccups.

"What are you doing to my wife?" Jesus Christ, it was Harmon.

"Your stupid wife . . ." Claude began.

Watch it, Claude, I remember thinking.

Sure enough, Harmon grabbed one of my arms and jerked me out of Claude's grip. I spun around and landed on the gravel path.

Harmon said, "Now what about my *stupid* wife?"

From my vantage point on the ground I looked up at the two men who were circling each other like hungry wolves. Harmon had three inches over Claude plus about eighty pounds. Their confrontation looked like it had been choreographed by someone with a bizarre sense of humor; Harmon in his western attire and Claude in his business pin-striped suit.

"Maybe you don't think it was so stupid for her to risk her life killing a German Nazi? Maybe you think it is all right because that is the way you do it in Oklahoma!"

Oh, ho. More than ol' Bonita Faye knocking off a German was in the works here.

"Bonita Faye never killed anybody in her life."

Oh, well. Just once, I thought.

"Oh, yeah?"

I was getting mixed up. Oh, yeah, was a line Harmon was supposed to use. Claude had been watching too many American gangster movies.

"Who? Who'd she kill?"

"Michel's father, that's who."

Harmon stopped his shuffle around Claude and

turned to look down at me. "Is that true, Bonita Faye? 'Cause if it isn't . . ."

He drew back his fist to show me what he was going to do to Claude if I hadn't really killed anybody.

"It's true," I said.

"Bonita Faye Adams! You killed a German Nazi?"

"Well, almost, Harmon. You see I was going to kill him, me and Simone, but Denis did it first. Shot him in the head out at the farm. But, it was my idea. . . ."

Harmon jerked me up off the ground and lifted me up in the air and shook me like Claude had . . . only harder. "You stupid woman . . . you idiot. Did it ever occur to you that you could get hurt or killed?" Harmon dropped me just like that and I fell into my previous position on the ground. His boots spit gravel in my face as he spun around to face Claude.

Harmon held out his hand. "Claude, I'm right sorry about *that.* . . ." His shrug indicated their former sparring area.

"It is all right, Harmon. I would have reacted in the same way. I had no right to shake Bonita Faye, but it was such a stupid thing for her and Simone to do. Here, have a cigar."

Harmon who hadn't smoked anything but an occasional pipe since Korea, took the cigar and waited while Claude lit it. Both men's hands were shaking and it took awhile for Harmon to get it lit. Then Claude lit his own cigar.

As quick as if the lighting ceremony had signaled a change of acts in a play, the two men began a different script.

"Now do you think you could explain all of this to me, Claude?"

"Surely can, Harmon."

"First, though, I need a drink. Do you know a good bar around here?"

"Matter of fact, I do. There is one right outside the park. I will consider it a pleasure to buy you a whiskey."

"Oh, no. I said it first. You're my guest."

Then those two gentlemen just flat turned and walked away, leaving me sitting in the gravel with a crushed rose in my hand.

TWENTY-NINE

I watched from my favorite seat in Patsy's kitchen as she put the last stack of Girl Scout Cookies into a large cardboard box. "Here, Bonita Faye. Let's eat this spare box of chocolate mint ones. I swear I don't know who ordered 'em. I hope Cherry appreciates all this." Her broad gesture indicated the room full of boxed orders of cookies.

With her mouth full of cookie, Patsy dotted the i's and crossed the t's of the last order. She looked up and grinned, little bits of chocolate crumbs falling from her mouth. Pointing her yellow pencil at me, she said, "You know. Show me a woman who can successfully be a Girl Scout Cookie Chairman and I'll show you a woman who can run the world."

Patsy is so smart.

She moved the paperwork aside and poured us both a fresh cup of coffee. Her first gulp washed away the crumbs and she reached for another handful. "Now, you were telling me about Didi."

"Not just about Didi. About going to her and Claude's home in Geneva."

"Were you over being mad at him and Harmon then?"

I said I had been, and I guess that was the truth.

It had been way after supper the day they had left me sprawled in the park before the two of them came home drunk as lords.

I hadn't even pretended to be asleep when Harmon staggered into our room. I was sitting, propped up by all the pillows in the center of the bed. My low cut, sleeveless gown showed off the bruises on my crossed arms. As he stumbled around, trying to pull off his clothes, I gave him one of Mama's looks. You know, one of those looks that don't require any words to let you know of your low standing in the community.

Naked, Harmon half fell onto the bed. "Poor Bonita Faye. Did I do that to you?" His big fingers outlined the blue marks on my arm. "I'm so sorry, sweetheart."

"Don't you sweetheart me, Harmon Adams. You've never hurt me before in my life and I can't just forget about it with sweet talk."

"And I'll never do it again," he promised. Then he drew back a bit, "But, goddamn it, Bonita Faye. How on earth did you think you could do something as dangerous as killing a German Nazi? No wonder I went berserk."

"I didn't kill him. Denis did."

"Same difference. You planned it. I'm just glad you didn't do it in my jurisdiction. Imagine having to arrest my own wife for murder."

I decided to forgive him then before his thoughts went on in that vein. I put my arm around his shoulder and caressed his muscled neck.

"That's better." He pulled the gown from my shoulders and slipped his hand below my breasts. He whispered into my ear, "Hey, Bonita Faye, you're getting a little weight on your ribs."

I swatted his hand away and he moved it to a better place.

* * *

As I told Patsy, Claude and Didi's home in Geneva was more than you could ever imagine a royal palace to be. It was a perfect Swiss chateau overlooking one of the best views of Lake Geneva. And it was furnished with French period furniture of the kind that before I had seen only at Versailles. It was beautiful and I told her so.

"Thank you, Bonita Faye. Coming from you, that is a real compliment. Claude values your opinion so highly. He chose the house, but he left the decoration entirely up to me. I think it is nice, but I am always happy to hear someone confirm it. Claude seems happy here. Do you agree?"

We looked out of the French doors to where Claude and Harmon sat on the wide marble terrace, enjoying their cigars and an animated conversation. The Vermeillon's English nanny sat on the far steps and held Francois while petite Belle played at the foot of the formal gardens at the left of the terrace. Ever so often she ran up the stairs to give her father a feather or some other treasure she'd found in her play. Claude would stop his conversation and give the child a hug and kiss before she ran off again.

I answered Didi slowly. "In fact, Didi, I more than agree. Now that I've been here, I can't imagine Claude in any other setting or with any other woman."

She clasped my right hand in both of hers. "Thank you, Bonita Faye. Again, I think you know how much your approval means to me. And I am glad that you are the other woman that Claude loves."

I drew my hand back in surprise.

"It is all right. I know all about it. Claude told me before he proposed. At first, I was jealous of an unknown, perfect Bonita Faye, whoever she might be. Then as the years went by and Claude was so good to me and our children . . . I must confess, though, I was nervous about your coming back to France. Simone told me not to worry. That everything would be all right and she was right. I have seen how much you love your Harmon and it is good to know that you are the one who also loves my Claude. We Europeans understand such things, but do you know? I think Harmon understands, too."

Whatever.

Didi wasn't the only one who could give out compliments. I asked her, "Tell me, how do you do it? This big house, servants, children, and Claude is so demanding of your time. Yet, you seem so serene through it all. You're everywhere, but you're never harassed or frazzled about nothing. How do you do it, Didi?" I really wanted to know her secret.

"Well, first this was how I was reared. This is the type of life I am accustomed to living. All this was expected of me. But, mostly I draw strength from my religion. You know that I am Catholic?"

Well, now I hadn't. I didn't know much about Catholics. There wasn't a Catholic church in all of eastern Oklahoma that I knew of. The nearest ones were in Fort Smith across the Arkansas border. And all I remembered of them were the stained glass windows and the black-clad nuns from the convent that I often saw on the streets there. So I answered in the only way I knew about religion.

"You mean faith from the Scriptures? Do you read your Bible a lot? My best friend, Patsy, in Poteau knows it by heart."

"No, not really, Bonita Faye. Catholics aren't encouraged to read the Scriptures. We derive our comfort from the rituals and sacraments of the church itself. The sisters tell us how we must conduct ourselves and the priests hear our confessions and read the Holy Scripture. There is a beautiful, well-ordered rhythm to our religion."

I began to understand the orchestrated life I had

observed at the Vermeillons. Still I protested, "But what do you do when things go bad on you? How do you cope when Belle is sick, and Francois is crying, and the help quits, and Claude is gone . . . and . . . and you have a headache?" I'd tried to think of what the people around here would call a catastrophe.

I think Didi got the general idea. She answered, "Why, then I just offer it up."

"Offer what up? Who to?"

"Why, to God. When things are beyond my control, I say the right prayers and offer up the problems for God to solve."

And here all this time I thought I had to go to God and tell him the solutions, even murder, I had come up with for my own problems. Maybe this Catholic business wasn't all bad.

I was pondering on that, sitting on the same steps where the nanny had perched when I overheard Harmon and Claude on the terrace.

"When do you think you will go to Washington, Harmon?"

"Not long after we get back to the States. The next classes start around Labor Day. That's the first Monday in September."

"What has made you so interested in the FBI?"

"Actually this is the criminal investigation end of the Bureau. Solving crimes through evidence has always appealed to me. There's been many a time in LeFlore County when I wish I, or anybody for that matter, knew more about criminology. There's a lot of crimes go unsolved, Claude, for lack of proper evidence. Why, I remember when I met Bonita Faye, when her no-good husband was killed? That case has always bothered me. I've always thought there was more to it than . . . but, no never mind. They pinned it on someone and he's dead . . . was already dead when they found out he did it, so it's a closed case. But, I've always wondered. . . ."

Great. Now I had to ponder not only on the Catholic

church, but also on whatever it was that Harmon was up to and had seen fit to share with Claude and not with me.

"And they really have gold angels around their mirrors and holdin' up their clocks and all?" No matter how much I told Patsy about Claude and Didi's home, she always wanted to hear more.

"They call them cherubs. They're baby angels. But they're gold all right." We were clearing away the remains of our stolen chocolate treat when all the kids came flyin' in the kitchen. They started rummaging through the neatly stacked boxes, looking for a stray cookie.

"Mama, can I have one?"

"Me, too."

"And me. I want a cookie."

"Bonita Faye, *je voudrais la confiserie, s'il vous plait?*"

"Here. Here. I saved another box for y'all. You'll get some, too, Michel, but I wish you'd ask for it in English. I know you can speak it." Patsy took an unopened box of cookies from the cabinet and threw them up in the air. Sixteen tanned arms reached up at the same time and the box was tossed around the kitchen like a basketball. Finally Harry got a good hold on it and ran out of the kitchen with the others yelling and pushing behind him.

I laughed. "You know he does most of the time, Patsy. And I thought Michel was teaching you French?"

"He is." She spread her legs apart in a solid stance, put her hands on her hips and said, *"Parle vous Francaise? Chevrolet coupe?"*

"Oh, you." I laughed.

THIRTY

It was during their long talks over coffee in the Hotel Regina dining room that Simone and Harmon worked out our adopting Michel and bringing him home to Poteau. I knew what was going on, but stayed out of their way. They both knew how I felt and there was no sense in beating the issue to death.

But all three of us were present when we asked Michel.

He stared at his mother for a long time and then turned to face Harmon and me. "*Oui*, this will be a hard matter for the heart, but it will be the best for all of us."

After that unexpected adult reaction, he lapsed into being a little boy. At times he held on to his mother like a three-year-old and at others, he refused to acknowledge her presence.

I was that proud of Simone, and I think I got a glimpse of the calm state of mind and action that she musta used during the war to get through her work with Michel's father. Robert and Denis were supportive of her decision, had in fact, helped her to make it, but I felt that all three of them believed that they had failed in some way.

Robert and I talked about it often during the four extra weeks I stayed in France to complete the necessary paperwork. Harmon had returned to America after his vacation time expired.

"Bonita Faye, do you think the effects of this terrible war will ever end?" It wasn't like Robert to be so down.

I didn't have any bright reassurances to offer him.

After Harmon's departure, I had moved into my old van Gogh room; there was no sense in Simone losing the money the suite could bring in and, besides, I loved that room so much.

As I lay alone on my soft, narrow bed, I wondered how we had all come to be where we were. How had an ignorant girl from Oklahoma come to be a part of the lives of a family in Paris, France? And where was that ignorant girl anyway?

I could remember the hard years with Mama and the harder ones with Billy Roy, but it seemed to me that when Denis Denfert had first opened that taxi door for a visitor from America, it was for more than a ride in a taxi that I'd stepped into

Here I was married to an up-and-comer from Oklahoma who loved only me, and I also coulda been married to a man who was fixing to be one of the richest men in Europe. And who loved me. In fact, as I was thinking on all this, I could hear his footsteps in the hall, stopping at my door for a minute, before moving on.

Mama used to tell me that the difference in lettin' life happen to you or makin' life happen for you was in the heart. "If it don't feel good all the way to your heart, then do something to change it, Bonita Faye. Life's too short to have to carry around a heavy heart full of regrets." Mama had been better at preachin' it than livin' it.

Well, I had sure changed my direction that night on Cavanal Hill when I pulled that trigger on Billy Roy, and while I don't think murder was exactly what Mama had in mind, I hadn't hesitated then or since to make a decision that didn't feel right.

My heart ached for Simone; letting her son go to America hurt her bad. But, her lack of making a judgment call between Denis and Robert was making more sense to me. I could only guess about what went on in their three bedrooms on the second floor, but it musta felt right in all their hearts, 'cause when they were together, I never saw any signs of resentment or jealousy. Robert was Denis's best friend and Denis was his. And Simone fussed over them both. Maybe they were on a schedule like the Paris Metro and if they missed one train, they just patiently waited for the next.

It was cool for a summer night in France and I slid under my eyelet-covered duvet and pondered some more on who we all were while I pulled the petals from the red rose I had found on my pillow. When I woke up the next morning I was surrounded by the sweet aroma of the dried petals.

THIRTY-ONE

Harmon had never been as happy being sheriff of LeFlore County as he thought he would be. "They never did want no honest sheriff," he'd come home and tell me, "they just wanted a hero to show off."

He'd kept on trying though.

"You know what Bennett, that newcomer from Fort Smith, told me today?" he asked. "You know, the man who bought the Fowler land east of Poteau for his retirement? He said that last Saturday when he visited his property that a man in a pickup drove up and welcomed him to the county and then asked him if he was going to build on it. And did Bennett know that the Fowler land was part of the deer hunting area?

"Then afore the dust from his truck had settled, another one pulled into the field and told him to be careful of how he built 'cause there was lots of fires in this part of the state. And later on, another pickup with two men stopped by and asked Bennett if he was going to build a house there and disturb the deer. They said the last owner had been burned out and they warned

187

Bennett to build out of stone or brick 'cause it was an awful fire area.

"Bennett came to see me, not 'cause he thought I could do anything about it, but just to tell me why he had put the property back up for sale. Now, Bonita Faye, none of them men said anything wrong. No real threats or anything, but their message was loud and clear; leave the land alone or get burned out.

"And, what's worse, that's only the tip of the iceberg. Eastern Oklahomans have their own law and they want to keep it that way. Oh, we can ticket the speeders and clean up after a car crash and direct traffic, but when it comes to the gambling and the dirty deals, it's Katy-bar-the-door on real law enforcement.

"I want to do the job right, but when even the victims refuse to cooperate, it isn't easy."

Harmon kept on trying for about six years after we brought Michel home, but he only got real satisfaction from the criminology end of the job. He attended every criminology school the FBI put on and his reputation for solving crimes with a microscope instead of a gun is why the governor appointed him to be the head of the Oklahoma State Bureau of Investigation in 1963.

That's when we moved to Oklahoma City, or rather Harmon did. I stayed for Michel to finish his last year of high school before I joined Harmon. It took me that long to work up to moving away from Poteau.

I didn't ever feel like I was Michel's mother and he didn't either. He had a mother and we visited her every summer. I'd take him to Paris and after a good visit with the Vermeillons, I would travel around Europe, either on my own or with Robert or with whichever one of Patsy's kids I'd taken with me that year. I couldn't ever get Patsy to go.

Harmon wasn't Michel's father figure either.

Michel found his own father image and no one was more surprised than Jerry by the time we all realized that

Michel had adopted him to be the one he most admired. Oh, Michel and Harmon loved and respected each other and Harmon certainly could make that boy mind, but it was Patsy's husband that Michel followed around during his free time.

The two of them would climb houses and nail shingles in the hottest weather and never even sweat. And they'd build fences and paint barns and never say three words the whole time it took for the job. I'd have to shake Michel to say more than "Yep" or "Nope," after he'd been with Jerry. "At least, you can say 'yep, ma'am,' to me," I'd rave.

"Yep, ma'am," he'd say then, and grin and duck when I'd throw the newspaper or something at him.

He was a good boy and got along well with the other kids at school. Some made fun of his accent at first, but since everybody talks funny in Oklahoma anyway, it was soon overlooked and Michel was just one of the gang which is what he always wanted to be.

The only time I ever saw someone being ugly to him was not too long after Michel arrived in Poteau. It happened when Michel and I were out shopping. It was a rainy afternoon and we were just about to head for home when I decided I had better go to the bathroom before we ran five blocks home through the cold, heavy drops. I headed toward the one at the bank. There wasn't one inside. It was around the corner to the second door on the street. Only the bank workers and customers knew which door led to the restrooms inside and I was there in the Ladies when I heard an awful commotion outside.

"Frenchy, Frenchy. Parly voo yourself. Come on. Say somethin', frog."

I charged out of that restroom and found a spiderlike boy on top of Michel. They were both wallering around in the mud. All I had with me was my umbrella so I poked the boy in the ribs and told him in no uncertain terms to get off Michel and a few other choice words. The boy flashed me a devilish grin, kicked Michel one more time below the knee and ran around the corner into the bank.

"I coulda taken care of him, Bonita Faye. You didn't have to do that," Michel said.

"Who was that boy? Has he ever bothered you before? Do any of the other kids act like that?" I may not have been Michel's mother, but I sure knew how to act like one.

"No, he's the only one. But, don't worry about him. He's a little bully and doesn't have any friends. No one pays any attention to him. For God's sake, Bonita Faye, that boy is younger than I am. He just caught me by surprise and I slipped in the mud. You didn't give me time to get at him." Michel was embarrassed.

I didn't care. "Who is he?" I asked again.

"Baron Falkenberry."

The Judge's grandson. I shoulda known.

Michel never mentioned him again, but I'd hear from time to time about how the Falkenberry boy would get in some kind of trouble. I told Harmon that one of these days he'd be dealing with that boy himself.

But I'll say this for Poteau, for the most part, Michel fit in just like any other kid, going to school, playing sports, kissing the girls, and doing chores around the house.

The chore Michel liked the most that he and Jerry did together was gardening and they'd work forever on someone's lawn, getting it just perfect, not even knowing that it was suppertime or that the sun had set.

I hired them both to work on my yard. Other than mowing, it hadn't had a lick of work done on it since Billy Roy and I had moved into it.

At first, Harmon had wanted to build us a new house, but you know how stubborn I can be. So we just fixed up the old one. We added another bath and modernized the kitchen. And built on a den and a fireplace. But to me it was the same old comfortable house. I could still sit on my front porch and swing while I read or just stare at the Oklahoma hills if I just wanted to think and sort out things.

It embarrassed me some when I realized I hadn't done much about the yard when Michel brought home a rose bush that Jerry had given him. No one loved flowers more than I did, but I guess I didn't know I could have them for my own.

"This is the kind of rose that you and Uncle Claude love so much," he told me as he dug a hole by the front porch.

"Wait a minute, Michel." I ran inside the house and got the old hatbox Simone had given me to save my rose petals in. When the hole was ready, I poured the dried petals in the bottom where the roots of the new bush would rest. "Seems right," was all I'd say in answer to Michel's questioning look. "How about you and Jerry plantin' me some more of those roses and, maybe, daisies, too?"

When I turned those two loose in my yard, it was like rain in the desert. I had something blooming almost every day of the year and if it weren't blooming, it looked pretty and smelled good.

Why, Michel almost didn't go with me to France the year after he graduated 'cause some of his best flowers were coming up. He wanted to know why Simone couldn't come to us again that year and, if I hadn't taken Sary and Omega along, I don't think I'd ever got him to go. Patsy and I knew that Michel would go anywhere that Sary went. When he wasn't following Jerry around, we could always find him at Patsy's daughter's side.

Simone and I didn't let them get married in France. That wouldn't have been fair to Patsy. So we all trooped back to Poteau and Sary and Michel were married in my garden with Sary holding a bouquet of Michel's last blooms of the summer.

I let them have the house when I moved to Oklahoma City.

You can't put a brick on their heads or anchors on

their legs to keep kids from growing up and every year more of them shot up and sprouted wings.

Harry and Cherry went to law school. Mary became a doctor and went to Vietnam. Jerry, Jr., took over the Poteau bank after the Judge died and Carrie was principal at a high school in Texas. Michel and Sary had babies, and Omega followed his older brother and sister to law school and wound up being the youngest U.S. Senator ever elected in Oklahoma.

Every one of those kids paid me back every cent I had loaned them for their education.

And, oh, yes, Elly Ross married a geologist and moved to Albuquerque, New Mexico.

THIRTY-TWO

You don't have to read this part if you don't
want to. There's some boring stuff about how
Harmon and me lived in Oklahoma City, Oklahoma, and some bad things you might not like. I know
I didn't, but they happened all the same so they got to be
wrote down. That Bible verse Patsy and me were so
keen about says, "Write it down," and I've tried to be true
to it ever since, even when it hurts to tell.

I get so caught up telling about how much Claude and
I loved each other, that sometimes I don't think I've
rightly told about Harmon and me.

Claude was easy to love. He was dark, handsome,
romantic, and French. And, true to his callin' it, very
riche-riche.

Harmon was different, but at the same time, I can see
now that both men shared some likeness. And not in just
loving me, either. They were both good men, honest to
a fault, and had the git and go to get where they wanted
to be. Claude darted back and forth like a blue-bottle
fly over a pond, but Harmon pushed on like he was

dancing the Oklahoma Shuffle; first on one foot and then on the other.

Harmon was handsome, too, in a raw-boned rangy fashion that filled out to one impressive man as we got older. He wasn't romantic in the French way, but in Harmon's way. After telling me he loved me a few times, he just took it for granted that I knew it, so the subject didn't come up all that often.

And I could count on one hand the number of times he sent me flowers, but I remember him on his hands and knees many a time, gathering wildflowers for me on our walks in the country.

Looking back, I see where I coulda been a better wife to him. Instead of high-tailing it back to Poteau every chance I got or over to France, I coulda shown up for more of those dinners and meetings and things where the wife was asked to come. I went to a lot of them though and even learned to sit through the worst without having to leave the head table to go to the bathroom more than once.

One of the "Ladies' Days" where I got to go with him stands out in my mind. Even if I hadn't been allowed, I would have gone. Harmon and I drove down from Oklahoma City to Heavener where they were dedicating the Heavener Runestone State Park. Him talking about the runestone and a future state park at a Poteau town meeting was where I had first seen Harmon, and it was a sentimental trip for both of us.

It was in October of 1970 and the trees had already turned, had already pulled back their green chlorophyll to let nature's real colors show through and it was like descending into a Thanksgiving basket as the official group of us wound our way down into the ravine that held the great stone.

Harmon and I grinned and held on to each other on the steps. I had begun to suffer twinges of arthritis in my knees and he still had a slight limp left over from Korea. "Aren't we a fine pair to be thinking we can go climbing down this mountain. It'd better be worth it, Harmon Adams, 'cause I'm never going to do it again," I told him.

The symbols on the runestone are supposed to be a Norse cryptopuzzle hiding the date of sometime in 1012, but as we stood there gazing up at it, securely protected by an ugly, twelve-foot steel cage, Harmon musta been feeling his oats, 'cause he whispered in my ear during one of the speeches, "It really says 'Harmon Adams Loves Bonita Faye and Don't You Ever Forget It.' "

I never have forgotten that or how Harmon held my hand all through the Lions Club luncheon that day at the Black Angus in Poteau, not letting go even when he had to stand up and be recognized as one of the people who had been pushing for the park in Heavener for years.

I liked the American Legion meetings the best. There's something prideful about seeing all those old men in their uniforms, and all that red, white, and blue crepe paper. And when one of them would die, they'd play taps. There's nothin' sadder or prettier than taps.

We had a nice home in Oklahoma City. Two-story and brick and all. With the kids from Poteau going to the University of Oklahoma down the road in Norman and running up for weekends, the bedrooms were full most of the time.

"Who's here now, Bonita Faye?" Harmon would ask when we sat down to supper and there'd be three or four plates set.

"Harry and a friend of his from Tulsa. They're just eatin' and runnin'. There's some kind of rock concert in town." Or, "Sary and the baby. She was lonesome for Michel while he's away at that agriculture meeting and Patsy sent her up here to mope around. Patsy said she was sick and tired of Sary cryin' all day to her. By the way, you got to put the baby bed back up in her room."

"We might as well just leave the dang thing up all the time."

All the kids that cluttered up our house and our lives weren't all Patsy's or even Michel's. Harmon never forgot what a helping hand meant to a boy who was alone and who felt like the whole world was against him. Time after time, he'd bring by some boy for "a good meal" or "just to spend one night."

One of them, a half-breed from eastern Oklahoma showed up one day as much in need of a bath as a meal. Harmon held him by the neck of his dirty blue-jean jacket and told me, "This is R.J. Walker. He'll be staying the night and he's hungry."

I said, "And I'll be feeding him just as soon as you show him the bathroom and what soap is for, Harmon."

That hot bath washed away some of the belligerence I had detected in the fifteen-year-old and when he sat down to the kitchen table in one of Harmon's bathrobes, all that was left in his dark brown eyes was an old tiredness.

After he'd eaten and gone to bed, Harmon told me R.J.'s story. "He's an orphan. Has been for several years. He's gone from one foster home to another." Harmon sighed. "It's an old story, Bonita Faye. We just throw away our kids . . . leave them on their own until they do something we can punish them for . . . and we say it's all their fault. This one was caught stealing something to eat from the 7-Eleven."

"What's going to happen to him?"

"I don't know. I'll find out tomorrow."

During the night, I heard a strange noise coming from the room where R.J. slept. I got up without waking Harmon and went in to see the boy. He was asleep . . . dead to the world . . . but tears were running down his cheeks and every so often, he'd sob.

The next morning at breakfast Harmon said, "Bonita Faye, I've been thinking. . . ."

"Yeah, me, too, Harmon." I buttered his toast.

"Maybe we could . . ."

"Yeah, I reckon we could." I poured his coffee.

R.J. stayed with us for three years until he went off to Carl Albert Junior College in Poteau. One of the delights of my life was seeing the light begin to shine in his eyes. He was a good boy and a good student. And Harmon was his own personal hero. After his graduation from Carl Albert, R.J. joined the state police 'cause he wanted to be a trooper like Harmon had been.

A lot of boys came and went in those years, but R.J. Walker was the only one who became family.

Harmon never seemed to mind that we didn't ever have any babies of our own and that was good 'cause while I woulda if I'd had to, I was just as glad to skip that part of being a woman.

And he didn't give no never mind to my gaining weight either. Least he never said so in front of me. In fact, he always acted like he liked having more of me around to cuddle. I'd hear him brag to some of his friends on poker playing night, "No, sir. Never had to get me a divorce like Joe here to get me a new woman. I just grew one. I'll bet you Bonita Faye has more than doubled her weight since we married."

I had to think on it real hard to make a compliment out of that one.

But I knew what he meant. Now, I wasn't "waddle-down-the aisles" fat, but I had put on a little meat from the time when I was Billy Roy's skinny little widow woman.

The only time Harmon and I ever argued was about money . . . my money. Over the years, the revenue from my "French Joint Venture" continued to mount up. It represented only a very small part of Claude's holdings and I think he really held on to the souvenir business only because of me and Denis. Denis had turned the company into a quality enterprise. He dealt only in the finest products and opened his own kiosks throughout France. With the increase in tourism in Europe, it was quite a profitable venture for all of us. Harmon didn't mind if I spent the money on the kids' education . . . in fact, he was glad I did . . . but the lines were clearly drawn about what I could use the French money for and what I had to spend his on. Tuition, room and board, books, and trips to Europe were okay, but Christmas and birthday gifts, furniture and clothes came from his account.

Going back to Paris, France, was not on Harmon's priority list. He'd enjoyed his one visit and sometimes talked about France like he had been born there, but once he'd seen it, he didn't ever care to go again. Or any of the other places that we took Michel, and later R.J., on their spring vacations from school. Not back to Washington, D.C., or the Grand Canyon or Disneyland or none of the other U.S.A. vacation spots. So the kids and I always picked someplace new each spring to visit and every summer Michel and I headed to Europe, leaving Harmon on his own to fish or play cards or whatever. After R.J. came into our lives, he was company for Harmon. R.J. never did want to go to France. Harmon always told people I was away visiting relatives and in a way, I guess I was. Next to Patsy and R.J., the Vermeillons were the only family I had outside of Harmon himself.

Harmon would go with me to Poteau for holidays though and we'd stay in the guest room in our own house or up at the big house the kids had built for Patsy and Jerry. It was a pale pink brick with the second-most beautiful yard in town. Visitors thought it must belong to the mayor and were always surprised that it was the local handyman's home.

Harmon and I "got by" in a way that Mama woulda been proud of. I loved the bigness of him, the way the silver shown in his brown hair and the way I knew he loved me every day whether he took the time to say so or not. He'd burst in the house evenings and shout, "Bonita Faye?" And when I'd say, "In the bedroom, Harmon," or, "out here in the den, Harmon," he'd follow me around until we'd wind up at the kitchen table drinking coffee while he told me about his day.

I like to think all that adds up to real love.

I was expecting him home early one spring day in

1985 when I heard the front door open. I waited for Harmon's call so I could tell him I was in the kitchen, but it was Omega's voice who called, "Bonita Faye?"

"In the kitchen, Omega. What are you doin' here? Can you stay for supper? Harmon and I are just goin' to have a light one. We're supposed to be watching our weight."

Well, sir, when that boy who was a United States Senator walked into my kitchen, I knew. Some things just don't have to be told with words if you know how to read someone's face. I sat down heavy on a kitchen chair and said, "Tell me about it, Omega."

This is how Omega told it to me, and how I'm tellin' it to you.

"There was this kid that was supposed to be transferred from the county jail to McAlester. And you know how Harmon always took time to talk to country boys gone bad? You know how he always said, 'I was raised up hard, too, and but for the Grace of God, I coulda ended up going down the other road?'

"Well, Harmon had heard about this boy and said he would take him down to the state pen himself if the sheriff didn't mind. So Harmon and a deputy took him down there. The deputy drove and Harmon rode in the back with the boy. This wasn't just one of your ordinary kids in trouble. He'd killed a man and was on drugs before he was arrested.

"The kid went crazy when they got to McAlester and got the deputy's gun. He was waving it around and talking out of his head. Harmon coulda shot him, but he never even went for his gun. The boy shot him in the heart and Harmon died instantly."

Harmon always said he'd never kill again.

We buried Harmon in the national cemetery in Fort Smith, Arkansas. Someone from the American Legion played taps and the wind blew the flags set up for

Memorial Day. Everywhere you looked, there was the red, white, and blue waving in the spring breeze. It was the most beautiful and the saddest day of my life and I never want to talk about it again.

THIRTY-THREE

COUNTY SHERIFF DENIES REOPENING
FOUR-DECADE-OLD MURDER CASE

The LeFlore County Sheriff's department today denied that they are re-opening a 40-year-old murder case at the request of an accused killer's grand-daughter. Sheriff's deputy Johnny Stovall admitted that Elizabeth Jenkins, granddaughter of Steuben Ross, has requested that the case against her grand-father be re-examined. Ross was accused of killing Poteau businessman Billy Roy Burnett in September of 1950.

The Winslow, Ark., na-tive died in a freak truck accident before he could be charged with Burnett's murder, but the murder weapon found in the bed of Ross's truck led authorities in both Oklahoma and Arkansas to conclude that Ross had shot Burnett on Cavanal Hill and the case was closed.

Now, 20-year-old Eliza-beth Jenkins of Albu-querque, N.M., has revealed to the police that her mother, Ellen Ross, later adopted by Fayetteville professor H.B. Abernathy, repeatedly stated before her death earlier this month that her father, Steuben Ross, was inno-cent. Ellen Ross was four years old when the moth-erless child accompanied her father up on Cavanal

Hill in the fall of 1950, the night Ross supposedly shot Burnett.

"My mother told me about my grandfather, my real grandfather, before she died. She was only a baby, but she remembered going camping with her daddy and she says he didn't kill Mr. Burnett. She said there was someone else up on that hill that night," Jenkins said.

Poteau Sheriff Delbert Hoyle and Deputy Harmon Adams were the investigating officers on the case that was closed after Burnett's shotgun was found in Ross's wrecked truck bed. Ross died in an accident near Mountainburg, Ark., two days after Burnett's murder. Hoyle died in 1962 and Adams, who became head of the Oklahoma State Bureau of Investigation (OSBI), died five years ago at the hands of a deranged prisoner at McAlester State Penitentiary.

Adams's widow, Bonita Faye Adams, was married to the victim, Billy Roy Burnett, at the time of the murder. Mrs. Adams lives in Poteau, but was unavailable for comment about Jenkins's accusations.

Stovall said his office is investigating Jenkins's story, but so far there is not enough evidence to reopen the case.

Jenkins said that she also will continue to investigate the case. ∎

My phone rang.

"Bonita Faye? You're home. Have you read the paper?" It was Patsy. She was almost crying.

"I got home last night. I thought it was too late to call. Yes, I've just read the paper. What on earth is going on, Patsy?"

"I don't know. I swear to God, I don't know. I only got back from visiting with Carrie in Corpus yesterday myself. Is she really Elly's daughter? And, Bonita Faye, is it true? Is Elly dead?"

That was the hard part. I hadn't known that my little Elly was dead, had died somewhere out in the West while

I was in Hot Springs taking the mineral baths to ease my arthritis. I had been with Elly all her life, all her life that I had known of her until her marriage to Charles Jenkins in 1969. After that I had let her go and now she was dead, had died wondering about her real daddy. I had owed Elly and I had let her down.

I remembered the first time I had seen her. The moon had been bright up on Cavanal Hill and as I raced past an empty campsite, Billy Roy's shotgun still hot in my hand, I had seen the moon reflected in a pair of startled eyes. I had thought it was an animal, a raccoon maybe, but she whimpered in fright as I ran by, and I had seen that it was a little girl sitting alone on a rock in the path.

"It's all right," I whispered. "Someone will come for you." When I reached the bottom of the hill—when I finished my mad pell-mell charge down it—I hadn't associated the child with the truck full of firewood parked on the road. I had stopped to push my tangled, leaf-filled hair out of my face and I realized I still clutched the shotgun and had thrown it in the back of that pickup where it fell down among the stacked cords like the snake I had felt it to be in my hands.

I hadn't known that someone else would be accused of Billy Roy's murder—hadn't known that anyone but me would ever be suspected. That's why I reacted so violently when Sheriff Hoyle had sat in my kitchen and told me about little Elly Ross. I had been waiting for him to say it was me, and he went and said it was Elly's daddy that they thought killed Billy Roy.

You got to believe me when I say I would have confessed if Steuben Ross had still been alive . . . if Elly hadn't been already so settled in at Fayetteville in what seemed to be a better life for her. And I'd of told any time during those years that I kept watch over her through me and Patsy's network if there had ever been the slightest indication that child was suffering 'cause of my sin.

What had I missed?

What had I missed looking at Elly's school pictures, pouring over each one, trying to see inside her soul? What had I missed the year I had gotten up the nerve to meet her face to face in Fayetteville at the social get-together at the university?

I had convinced myself I had missed nothing, yet now I read in the Poteau paper that when my Elly lay dying away off in New Mexico that her soul was troubled and it was all because of what I done to her.

My phone rang.

It was a newspaper reporter from Fort Smith wanting to come out and talk to me about Billy Roy's murder.

I said come on ahead.

My phone rang.

It was a television reporter from Fort Smith who wanted to get me on a news program they was doing about Billy Roy. They was going up on Cavanal Hill and would I come along and be interviewed?

I said no, I wouldn't. The arthritis in my knees wouldn't let me climb mountains or hills any more, but to come on ahead to the house and I'd give them an interview.

My doorbell rang.

It was Elizabeth Jenkins, Elly's daughter.

She stood there in the doorway with her suitcase in her hand. It was one of them expensive flower-patterned kind that folds over on itself. Didi had brought the same kind of luggage when she had visited last.

That's what I saw. The suitcase and then the girl.

"Mrs. Adams? I'm Elizabeth Jenkins."

"Yes, I thought you might be. You look some like your mother."

"You knew my mother?"

"Yes, some."

"May I come in?"

Where were my manners? Of course, she could come in. As we settled down in the living room, Elizabeth's suitcase still in the front hall, I looked her over good. She did have some of the same look of Elly, but it was a fragile out-of-the-corner of your eye resemblance. As fragile as the girl herself.

Where Elly had been strong her daughter appeared delicate. Elly had thick, shiny brown hair, Elizabeth's was a fine blonde. Head on, eye to eye, there was nothing that would have made me stop in the street and exclaim, "Oh, I know you. You're Elly Ross's daughter." Elizabeth seemed a faint shadow of the vibrant young Elly I remembered, so frail that she didn't even seem able to bear up under the long name of Elizabeth.

"What did your mother call you?" I asked suddenly.

"Why, 'Libby.' But how did you know?"

Libby. Yes, she could be a 'Libby.' Elly knew she had overnamed her only child.

She was pretty though. But I was afraid to touch her . . . touch those small-boned arms with their fine white hands. Afraid she'd disappear, or worse, break, under my touch.

"Tell me about your mother. How she died."

The eyes, lighter than Elly's, filled with tears. "It was cancer. In one way, it was quick. In another, it was too long."

"She suffered then?"

"Yes, but I was with her all the time. My father and I. We stayed with her until she died."

"Was that when she told you about her daddy, Steuben Ross? I read about it in the paper."

"Yes, I knew my Mother was adopted. That the Abernathy's weren't my real grandparents. But, Mother never mentioned that she knew . . . that she remembered . . . anything about her real parents. Oh, not her mother, of course, but about her father. She told me about it when I sat with her at the hospital. The doctors said it was the drugs that made her remember. I don't know if she even realized what she was telling me. You can imagine how shocked I was to hear my real grandfather was an accused murderer."

The not quite Elly-child leaned forward. "What can you tell me, Mrs. Adams? What do you know about your first husband's murder that Mother didn't?"

THIRTY-FOUR

By the time the reporters came to the house, I had fed Libby a roast-beef sandwich, potato salad, milk, and chocolate cake at my kitchen table.

And I had come to a conclusion.

What I would of told Elly if she'd asked . . . what I might of told Harmon if he'd asked, I was not going to tell Libby. That child was not grieving for her dead grandfather, she was grieving for her dead mother and I couldn't give Elly back to her.

Before the reporters came, R.J. knocked at my kitchen door three times before walkin' on in like he always did. He knew that the evenings were the loneliest for me, the time I missed Harmon the most, so that was mostly when he'd drop by, to drink coffee and have a bite to eat with me. He'd tell me what was going on in the sheriff's department, and although I didn't really care, I'd listen and say the right words back. It was his coming by that meant so much to me, not the illegal goings-on in LeFlore County, Oklahoma.

Today it was hardly noon and there he was. As he

walked through the back door, I thought how handsome and strong he looked and how his Indian bloodline stood out more so than usual. Or it coulda been the contrast between him and the pale girl seated at the table.

"Howdy, R.J. You hungry? Sit down and I'll fix you a bite. R.J. this is Libby Jenkins. You might of read about her in the paper. Libby, this is my friend, R.J. Walker. He's our best deputy sheriff."

"Miz Jenkins."

"Deputy Walker."

R.J. sat down at the table across from Libby. "I'm glad I caught you here, Miz Jenkins. The sheriff wanted me to ask you a few more questions."

"All right," Libby answered in a low, soft voice.

"You say your mother saw someone else up on Cavanal Hill? Did she tell you who?"

Libby looked embarrassed. "She said . . . my mother said it was a fairy."

"Pardon?"

"A fairy. A fairy came out of the trees and told her not to cry. That her daddy was coming for her. And then the fairy disappeared. She was only four years old, Deputy."

"So what do you think she meant by that, Miz Jenkins? A fairy?"

"I think it means that there was someone up there. The real someone who killed Mrs. Adams's husband and who comforted my mother as *he* escaped."

R.J. wrote it down and then he surprised me by pulling out Sheriff Hoyle's old brown spiral Aladdin notebook. As he turned the pages, I noticed that they were still curled at the edges from the steam from the hot coffee I had poured the sheriff right here in this very kitchen forty years ago.

"We found this notebook in Billy Roy Burnett's murder file. It was in a box in a storeroom. I think you've covered everything in it with Sheriff Stovall 'cept we were wondering if your mother mentioned the bells."

"The bells?"

"Yes, these notes say Elly Ross reported hearing bells right before the gunshot. Did she mention that to you, Miz Jenkins?"

I busied myself at the counter, fixing a sandwich for R.J., but I heard Libby answer, "No, Mother never said anything to me about hearing any bells. Were they supposed to be cowbells or church bells? Or what?"

"I don't know. It just says 'bells' here in these notes. I guess it's not important." R.J. put the brown notebook away.

I'd always known what bells Elly had heard. Right before I shot Billy Roy, he'd laughed out loud and called my name, "Belle, Belle, Belle." That was right before he'd told me I wouldn't ever be going to no Paris, France. Right before he told me I'd have to sleep with the Judge the next time. Right before I pulled the trigger.

Billy Roy's loud cruel laughter musta swept through the trees like the ringing of the very object my name sounded like. The words musta rang loud and clear to a four year old only a few hundred yards below. If her daddy had heard . . . had seen anything . . . we'd never know.

I served R.J. his roast beef sandwich. "Do you want milk or iced tea with this, R.J?"

We gave the interviews together. Me and Elly's girl.

"Yes, I was surprised when Libby here showed up in Poteau."

"No, I didn't know anyone else was up there on Cavanal Hill when my first husband was killed."

"Yes, I met Harmon Adams during the investigation of the murder. We married almost three years later."

"Yes, Harmon was a fine man."

Libby didn't say much to the reporters. I think they were disappointed, but like I said in the beginning, it was just a little murder and the only interest they really had in the story was that the widow of the murdered man had married the investigating officer, a man who turned out to be a hero of eastern Oklahoma.

When I watched the television coverage later that night, there was more of Harmon and his famous shootout in Panama than there was of Libby's accusations. The TV pictures were good and clear, just like looking into my bathroom mirror: There I sat on my living room couch, an overweight, old country woman dressed in a serviceable plaid housedress, holding on to the hand of a beautiful pale girl who was suddenly shy and afraid of the spotlight.

Libby was so shook that after they all left, I took her into my guest room and had her lie down. She was already asleep, her fair hair covering the pillow, when I finished covering her with the colorful old afghan that lay at the foot of the bed.

I called Patsy.

"It's all right," I assured her. "It's a tempest in a teapot. No one is really serious about this investigation of Billy Roy's death. It'll blow over quick, just like it blew in." What Patsy and I hadn't ever talked about in forty years, we didn't talk about that night either.

I sat down in the rocker in the front room in the gathering darkness of a June twilight. Like R.J. knew, this was the hardest time of the day for me. This was the time when Harmon would come in and yell, "Bonita Faye, where are you?" It had been five years, but every evening I swear I could hear the echo of his call.

Sometimes I talked to him anyway. I did that night.

"Harmon, I'm right here. Right here in Poteau, Oklahoma, asitting in this rocker, wondering what in the world is going on. Right here in our little house that I've lived in since you know when." I still couldn't say "since you died."

Forgetting that I'd already told it before I said out loud to Harmon that Michel and Sary and their kids had moved to Paris, France. That Michel had been so worried about Simone after her heart attack that the whole kit-and-caboodle of them now lived on the farm outside Boulogne. Michel had built a fine farmhouse on the spot where the original garden had stood.

And did Harmon remember me atelling him about the French workman finding the bones of an unknown man under the garden soil? How they had a fine funeral for that man? How Simone had written that Michel never knew that he was shedding tears for his own father during the service? But, that somehow Michel had been easier with his own life since then?

I switched on the light next to the rocker. Its rays sent Harmon back into the shadows of the room.

"You old fool," I said to myself. Still, I whispered one more message to the corner of the room. "Harmon, Elly's daughter is alying in our guest bedroom. What am I going to do with her?"

THIRTY-FIVE

"**I** just couldn't stay on here, Mrs. Adams. I just couldn't," Libby told me the next morning when she'd finally woke from her deep sleep. Her voice was saying "no" but her body wasn't making any charge at the front door.

"Sure you can, Libby. Maybe not to find out about your grandfather, but to learn more about the place where your mother was born . . . where she grew up. Winslow and Fayetteville aren't that far away. I might be wrong, but I think that will help you through this time."

"I don't know, Mrs. Adams."

Poor child. She really didn't know what came next.

"Call me 'Bonita Faye.' And let's play it by ear. Stay here again tonight and we'll talk about it some more tomorrow. I like having company. It gets lonesome here at night."

"I guess I will then. My father doesn't need me. He's already planning to go to South America to conduct research for his company."

"Well, now, Libby, that's his way of handling your mother's death. You have to find your own way."

* * *

I was right.

The fuss about Billy Roy's murder and Steuben Ross's granddaughter soon died down. Only Miss Dorothy down at the nursing home still wanted to talk about it to me when I made my daily visit to her.

I might not of felt guilty about Billy Roy, but my cruel joke on Miss Dorothy haunted me all my life.

Miss Dorothy sat in a chair next to her bed in her private room that I paid for at the first of each month. Her hair was gray now, the home didn't color hair in their beauty shop, but she was still dressed in a yellow bathrobe. I had tried to bring her other colors, but she would only wear yellow.

The first time I winced over what I had done to Miss Dorothy was when Harmon and I were visiting from Oklahoma City and she came walkin' down Main Street in Poteau. After we had chatted and walked on, Harmon said, "Damn, Bonita Faye. That woman gives me the willies. And she's not that bad looking either. Or wouldn't be if she didn't always have that green hair and wear that godawful yellow."

As she got older and was forced to retire from her job, Miss Dorothy just got crazier. Little boys used to size up their manhood by daring one another to walk, not run past the "witch house," the small paint-starved cottage where Miss Dorothy lived. She'd come out on her front stoop and shake a broom at them, yelling obscenities while they tried to walk casually by on her cracked sidewalk. When she started coming out naked, is when they sent her to the nursing home.

Now Miss Dorothy sat in her wheelchair at the home and told me, "Bonita Faye, I think that Ross girl is on to something. I never did think her grandpa killed Billy Roy." The old woman glanced coyly at me out of the corner of her eyes. "You know Billy Roy and I were 'special' friends. You remember how he was partial to my pineapple upside-down cake, don't you?"

I didn't have to be arrested to be punished for Billy Roy's murder. I got a dose every day at two o'clock when I visited Miss Dorothy and she told me all about her love affair with my dead husband.

Miss Dorothy wasn't the only one in town who was interested in Libby Jenkins.

One day's stayover had led to another and by the time a month had passed, Libby was part of the Poteau social scene. Which wasn't much.

Poteau, Oklahoma, was as frozen in time as a dinosaur caught in an Arctic ice storm. Sometimes I thought the town had got stuck in the thirties and sometimes the fifties, but it had never gone much past its conception and it sure wasn't ready to face the last decade of the century. Don't get me wrong, that ain't all bad.

It was a nice, easy-going town where everybody was some kind of friend or enemy and it was clear which was which. There were no gray areas in Poteau. The people had an opinion on everything and you were either for or against something. You stood for one thing or you didn't. You were either Baptist or Church of God or you weren't. There were a handful of blacks in white.

I don't know where Libby met him. It coulda been at the Pay-and-Take It or maybe at the downtown corner drugstore, but you coulda knocked me over with a feather when one day late in summer, she came bringing home Baron Falkenberry.

The boy I'd pushed off Michel, the young man I had warned Harmon about, hadn't turned out any better than I'd first called it way back then. He said he owned a lumber yard, that he ran a creosote plant up near Panama. That he was rich and successful and somebody.

I knew better.

Oh, he was good-looking in a big, blond shiny way and he drove Libby home with her packages that first day in his red BMW convertible. That was enough to turn any girl's head, much less one as vulnerable as Libby Jenkins.

But I knew about Baron Falkenberry. As if being a Falkenberry himself wasn't bad enough, R.J. had told me about how Baron was being investigated for shady dealings and that maybe all of Baron's money didn't come from his business holdings. I knew that he was way older than Libby and that he'd been divorced twice. I remembered that as a teenager Baron had always tried to run with the older crowd and now that he was older, he had taken to hanging out with the younger ones where he played the hero, always paying for the booze and the good times.

There was even talk of him being involved in one of those Oklahoma murders where the accused always went free if he was a good ol' boy, or if he knew enough good ol' boys to help him. Or had enough money to pay his way out of jail time. Juries and justice go by another name in Oklahoma.

Baron brought in Libby's package as if it was as heavy as a bale of hay, when it didn't hold nothin' but a box of Kleenex, a pint of catsup, and a six-pack of Diet Cokes.

"Bonita Faye, you know Baron Falkenberry, don't you? He says he knows you. He was so nice to give me a lift home. And, guess what? Baron has invited me to go to Fort Smith tonight with him and some of his friends. Should I go? You know you're always telling me I ought to get out more."

What I thought was that it was a shame that ninny was an outdated word and if I'd called Libby that, she wouldn't even have known what I meant. Baron Falkenberry and I stared at each other over Libby's head, frozen grins on our faces and a declaration of open war in our eyes.

R.J. was disappointed when he learned that Libby was running around with Baron and his crowd. I thought I had detected an interest from him toward the girl, but he was too slow to act on it. And Libby treated him like a big brother who came around every day to tease and make her laugh. But there was more than just Libby that worried R.J. about Falkenberry.

"There's this investigation going on that involves him, Bonita Faye. I'm not free to say the details, but you'd better keep Libby away from him."

As if I could.

Libby wasn't dumb, she just wasn't smart about men. And at a time when she needed him the most, her father had up and taken off for South America. I didn't think much of the substitute Libby found for him.

She went out with Baron every night, staying later and coming home drunker each time. Then one night she didn't come home at all. She stumbled home right before noon the next day, defensive about her behavior. "I'm a grown woman, Bonita Faye. I know what I'm doing."

I didn't say anything 'cause I was afraid she'd move out and live with Baron altogether and I wouldn't get to be of any help to her atall. I don't know why she stayed on with me, probably 'cause she didn't have any place else to be. Her mama was dead and her daddy gone away. Maybe she knew she was better off at my house than full-time at Baron's.

I tried to talk to her, help her make plans for the future.

"Libby, are you going back to school in California this fall?"

"I don't know, Bonita Faye."

"Well, if you are, you'd better start thinking about registering. It's less than two months before the semester begins."

But I didn't ever see any signs that she was moving in that direction and the weeks slipped on by.

The morning she came to breakfast with dark bruises on her arms was too much for me. After we ate and Libby had gone back to bed, I drove up to Patsy's.

She had company.

I don't like to think that it was the money her kids sent that finally got Patsy accepted in Poteau. I like to think that the town . . . the church ladies in particular . . . learned to like Patsy for who she was and what she knew . . . about the Bible . . . and about faith . . . and about being good. Whatever it was, her house was always full of one woman or another atelling her their troubles and asking for advice. She'd come a long way from delivering the ironing to their back doors.

That day I had to wait for the preacher's wife to leave before Patsy and I could settle ourselves down in her kitchen in our old comfortable way.

"Have you lost weight, Bonita Faye?" was the first thing she asked.

"Maybe. Some. And if I have, it's worrying over that girl."

"Libby? What's she done now?"

"It's still Baron Falkenberry, Patsy. It's been almost three months and he's still hanging around. I don't know how much more time I've got before he steals her away altogether. Libby's bright enough. What do you think she sees in him? What attracts her to him? She could do better."

"I've been thinking on it ever since you told me about Baron and Libby, Bonita Faye. You know none of our kids turned out like her . . . not ever khowing the time of day or where to step to avoid the snakes in the grass. Our kids are all sensible." Patsy always gave me half credit for raising her children just like I did her with Michel and R.J.

"Maybe she had it too easy. She didn't have to come up the hard way like you and me. And, in some ways, even our kids. We always knew our next meal or our next day's lodging depended on our getting out and scratching for it. Remember those days, Bonita Faye?" Patsy and I both looked around her comfortable, bright kitchen. Even after all these years, our living in houses furnished like catalogue showrooms still startled us.

"I remember, Patsy. I remember when I didn't have my own pot to pee in and worse. But, Libby didn't grow up that way. That's why I don't understand how she could take a shine to a lowlife like Baron Falkenberry."

"Like most kids her age, Libby had it too easy," she repeated.

"I don't think Elly ever intended her daughter to turn out like this," I said.

"No, probably not. But she did. Why don't you just let Libby go, Bonita Faye? Send her on her way, so she'll get away from that man."

"I can't. I remember what a safe place Simone and Claude made for me in Paris. I needed that time to grow up. I think Libby needs it, too."

"Well, Baron Falkenberry ain't no Claude."

"I know that. Nobody knows that better than me, but I still think I can help her. I owe Elly, and, besides, there's something strange about Baron. It's like he's playing some game with Libby, dragging her down a little bit more every day. And, listen up to this one, I don't think Libby is really the one the game is all about. Every time he picks her up at the house, it's like his eyes are saying something private to me. Patsy, I think it's *me* he's after."

That Tuesday after I talked to Patsy, Libby and Baron showed up at the house early in the afternoon. I was outside deadheading the roses when they drove up.

Libby seemed nervous.

I tossed some dead roses into a paper sack on the ground and asked, "What's up?"

"Baron and I . . . we . . . Bonita Faye, we're . . ."

"What Libby is trying to say, Mrs. Adams, is that Libby and I are planning to get married and we hope you'll be happy for us."

Libby was looking up at Baron with a dazed and besotted look on her face, but Baron was looking right at me with a dare in his eyes.

THIRTY-SIX

I sent Baron Falkenberry a postcard in a plain white envelope. It was a picture of the Heavener Runestone and the typed message read, "Meet me here Saturday at 6:30."

I didn't sign it.

It took some doing, but I got Libby invited to Fayetteville for a stayover on Saturday night with friends of Elly's. They were eager to see Libby, but she didn't want to go. She finally agreed just to shut me up.

I got to the park about five. There just wasn't any way around it. If I was going to walk down into that valley with my arthritis kickin' up like it was, I would have to have plenty of time for the hike.

Parking my car around the curve from the park office, as far away as I could and still be able to walk back to it, I took off down the steps to the bottom of the gorge that held the runestone. The park closed at five and I passed a few tourists comin' out along the path. I had checked license plates and knew they'd be long gone on their way out of state before Baron met me at the stone.

I blessed the park service as I held on to the strong

railing that led to the bottom. The descent was even more difficult than I had remembered it, but with sitting on the benches along the way and even once on the steps, I made it in about forty-five minutes. I was breathing hard, my heart was beating fast and I could feel the ache in my knees, but all-in-all I felt right proud of myself. As long as I didn't dwell on the return trip.

I even began to enjoy the fall leaves as I sat on the stone retaining wall by the brown wood building that now protected the Heavener landmark. The reds, yellows, and purples of the changing foliage was brilliant against the gray of the canyon and the green of the cedar trees. By six o'clock, I was alone and imagining what the Vikings would of thought of if they returned to their hidden valley. I was enjoying this fantasy, listening to the wind murmur in the trees and watching the shadows get longer, when I decided that I could probably see more of the leaves if I climbed up on the higher cliff above the runestone.

There was a path up to it, even steps, but no railings to hold on to. And I fell once. It took me almost ten minutes to catch my breath after that, but I finally reached the top. My heart was pumping out of my body and my head hurt so bad, I was dizzy.

But I was right. The view from the higher ledge was spectacular. Standing at the edge, I could see the runestone's protective shelter below me about 50 feet and a small rushing waterfall over to my left. I moved away from the unprotected edge of the bluff, but where I could still keep an eye on the lower path, and just stood there and let the Valley of the Vikings wash over me.

The air was turning cooler as the sun descended behind the mountain and the birds were singing last minute songs, fluttering from branch to branch, before nesting down for the night. I could smell the damp earth and the decay that had already begun in the fallen leaves. Though I was still gasping a little, my heart slowed down and I felt relaxed and peaceful.

Down below me I saw Baron Falkenberry reach the runestone plateau. He entered the tunnel-like building at one end and immediately came out the other side. I remember thinking that I bet he didn't even glance at the massive stone with its secret message as he passed by it.

He stood with his hands in his pocket and looked around, but not up.

"Yoo hoo. Baron. I'm up here."

It only took him about two minutes to bound up the steps I had labored up for over thirty. He was wearing blue jeans, a red Polo pullover jersey, and an aviator's brown leather jacket. Out in the open, even in the fading light, I could see that Baron was beginning to look a little long in the tooth, a little too old to be who he wanted to be.

"It *is* you. I thought it was you," he said when he reached the top, huffin' only a little bit.

"I thought you might," I answered.

"Well, let's get right to it, old woman. You want me to stay away from Libby, right?"

"Yes."

"But, why up here . . . or down here . . . on Poteau Mountain?" He made a sweeping gesture with his arm.

"Oh, I don't know. It seemed like a good idea at the time. But as you said, let's get right to it, Baron. Are you going to leave Libby alone?"

"Maybe," he said.

"How much?" I asked.

"How much you offering?"

I was right in feeling all along that part of Baron Falkenberry's interest with Elly had included a private game with me.

"Fifty thousand."

He laughed.

"One hundred thousand and that's it, Baron."

"Dear old Bonita Faye. You've got it all wrong. That's only the beginning."

"What do you mean?"

"I want the whole million."

"Million? What million?" My heart was starting to race again and my speech came out in gasps.

"The million my granddaddy said you have in your bank account from your love affair with that Frenchman in Paris."

Claude?

"That was business," I protested.

"Yeah, and I know what kind of business it was, too. My granddaddy used to say you were hot stuff when you were young. You and your fancy airs and your no account husband. My granddaddy said he always thought you had killed Burnett up on Cavanal Hill, but you sweet talked yourself out of it with Deputy Adams. And they went and found a dead man . . . an innocent dead man to blame for it and you got off scot-free. Well, now, sister, it's time to pay the piper."

I stood with my hand on my heart, willing it to slow down.

Baron went on, "I had forgotten about you, forgotten my dead granddaddy's old stories until Libby came to town. I figured you'd feel some guilt about her and want to rescue her from someone as wicked as me. That was all there was to it at first. Then she told me about the *bells* her mama had heard up on that hill the night your husband was killed." He grinned a wicked grin and bent his face down toward mine. "Bet I'm the only one left alive in Poteau that remembers that Billy Roy Burnett used to call you Belle when you'd strut your stuff for him in your black Paris nightgown. Yes, ma'am, my granddaddy used tell me some awful interesting stories about you. I especially liked the one where you ruined his bank by taking your whore money and moving it to Fort Smith. Lady, you might have fooled that supposedly smart detective husband of yours, but you didn't fool my grandpa, and, lady, guess what? You don't fool me either!"

Baron was spitting a little as he jabbered his hate-filled narrative and for the first time I felt a personal fear. He was so close to me, towering over me. I tried to translate his words, his fears, his anger. What? The Judge? The money? Revenge? That was what I had felt when Baron had hugged Libby tight to him and smiled at me. Smiled at me with his full lips, but not with his treacherous eyes.

I'd been standing on that slab of rock for almost an hour. If I didn't sit down soon, I'd faint. I had double vision in my eyes and I could feel the blood trickling down from where I'd gashed my knee when I'd fallen.

"I'd just about given up on you, Bonita Faye. Thought I'd be stuck with that girl. Then I thought that if I started roughing her up a bit . . . started talking about marriage, you'd take the bait. And I was right and here's the proof." He took the white envelope out of his breast pocket and held it in front of me. I could see the postcard inside.

I snatched it away from him.

"That's all right, you old bitch. You keep your little ol' postcard. It's all over for you." He turned and stared out into the park below us, both hands on his hips and a satisfied smile on his face like he had just bought the whole valley, runestone and all.

He said, "I'll take the million and I think I'll take the girl, too."

I don't know where a tired, fat old woman got the energy to do it, but I had the strength of ten strong men when I reached out both hands and pushed Baron Falkenberry off that bluff.

The shove almost propelled me off the side with him. I didn't really care, but at the last second, my momentum stopped and I crashed heavily onto the stone platform at the same time Baron struck the ground below.

There was no one about to hear his scream or the sound of him hitting the jutting rocks. When I crawled over and peered over the edge I could see him lying face-up in an unnatural sprawl, his head half submerged in the fast current from the waterfall. He wasn't moving. I couldn't tell if he was dead or not, but I knew that if I climbed down to find out that I'd die from a heart attack right beside him.

You didn't have to climb to the ledge I was on by the steps. They was only there if you wanted to visit the runestone first. You could also get back to the main path by a smoother, slightly graded incline that went around the valley. That's the way I chose to get out of the park when I could finally get to my feet. The adrenaline I'd felt when I shoved Baron was gone and I hurt in every bone in my body. It took me nearly two hours of stumbling and falling in the dark, clinging to mossy rocks and resting on cold flagstone steps, before I reached my car in the parking lot.

It was deserted 'cept for a red BMW parked near the top of the steps.

I was so tired I almost couldn't get my car door open. When I did, I just sat there.

My mind was a blank. My brain refused to work.

When it finally did, it was on the lowest level of man: self-preservation. With hands that were shaky, dirty, and bleeding, I turned the key in the ignition. I had to use my hand to maneuver my foot so that it reached the pedal. With a leg that was so stiff that I wasn't sure it was there below the knee, I stepped on the gas. I drove home.

The rest of the evening was a blur. Sometimes Harmon was besides me, but most of the time I was alone.

I remember taking a hot bath, clipping my broken fingernails, and bandaging my swollen knee. I remember sitting, shivering in my warm red robe, at the kitchen table drinking a cup of hot tea laced with brandy.

And I remember my last thoughts of that day as I dropped onto the bed—before I fell into a dreamless sleep—"Murder, like childbearing, should be left to the young."

THIRTY-SEVEN

I had worn an old polyester pantsuit up to Poteau Mountain to meet Baron Falkenberry. It was one of several that I had bought when they were in their heyday and I had thought they would be just the thing for my trips to Europe. The pantsuits had turned out to be hot, smelly, and uncomfortable, but I had brought them back home, washed them and hung them in the storage closet.

Sunday morning, I chose a powder blue one. With its wide pants leg, it was all I could get over the thick bandage on my swollen knee. Saturday's black pantsuit lay torn and crumpled behind the hot water closet in the hall.

I missed church, but at ten to twelve I entered the Black Angus Cafe for Sunday lunch, leaning heavily on one of Harmon's old canes. The waitress went through the buffet for me, calling out the selections. She brought the filled plate to my table near the front door.

As I ate, I looked around the Angus. The old red and black carpet was gone as was the leather and chrome stools around the counter. In fact, the counter was gone.

And like everywhere else in America, the Angus's new colors were shades of blue and mauve.

"Howdy, Bonita Faye. We missed you this morning."

"Howdy, Claudia Jean. Bubba. I couldn't make it today. My arthritis is acting up again."

The church couples filed by my table as they headed for the buffet. I howdy'd all of them and watched their faces as they ate.

These were good people, my neighbors. And if they chose to sit in mauve chairs and eat somebody else's cooking at Sunday noon, maybe it was just a sign that Poteau, Oklahoma, wasn't so far behind the rest of the country after all. Still, I thought, these were the women who twenty—even ten—years ago woulda been calling their families in to eat their Sunday fried chicken on their own polished dining-room tables.

Finally, the one I'd been waiting for showed up.

R.J. went to the back and poured himself his own cup of coffee before sitting down across from me.

"Bad news, Bonita Faye."

I didn't say nothing, just put a concerned look on my face.

"Baron Falkenberry fell off a cliff up on Poteau Mountain yesterday."

"No, you don't say, R.J."

"Yep, he won't be bothering Libby no more."

"Hurt bad, is he?"

"Worse than hurt. He's dead."

"Land's sake, R.J. Is that why you have on your uniform on a Sunday morning? You investigating his death?"

R.J. poured extra sugar into his cup.

"Well, yes and no," he said mysteriously.

"I don't follow you, R.J."

"I've been up all night, Bonita Faye. Working on something that involved Baron Falkenberry alright, but not his death. We didn't find out about that until about two hours ago when the park opened. It's a shame he died when he did."

"Why's that?"

He pulled out a white legal paper from his back pocket. It was creased where he'd sat on it. "This is a warrant for Falkenberry's arrest." He threw it on the table. "Guess I won't need it now."

"Arrest for what."

"We raided his place last night. Up near Panama? Found eight different marijuana patches up on that ranch of his. The high quality kind that would bring top dollar. And everyone of them was booby-trapped, too."

"No."

"And that's not all. He had an airstrip . . . for light planes . . . in one of his back pastures. One of the state helicopters spotted it from the air a couple of weeks ago. That's when we stepped up our investigation. We think there was also some cocaine dealing going on. And worse."

"Worse than cocaine?"

"Yep. The dogs went crazy out around one of the sheds in Falkenberry's woods. We started digging . . . those dogs are trained to find drugs . . . and we uncovered some bones . . . human skeletons, Bonita Faye."

"Lordy, R.J."

"There's some people from Harmon's old crime lab in Oklahoma City up there right now trying to figure out how many and who they are."

"Well, what do you think of that?"

"But, that isn't what I came in here to see you about, Bonita Faye. I'm afraid I've got to ask you some questions."

Well, didn't I know it. And here I thought I could get by with another murder. Like Billy Roy's, it was just a little one and I only killed every forty years or so. I figured I'd be dead by the next time the urge hit me.

I had to wait for R.J. to get himself another cup of coffee. And he stopped by the buffet and picked up a piece of pecan pie. I began to feel a little better. A man can't sit and eat pecan pie while's he's arresting you for murder, can he?

"Bonita Faye, someone saw your car up at the Heavener State Park yesterday."

"That's right, R.J."

"May I ask what you were doing up there?"

"Looking at the fall leaves. You know they turn first down in that ravine, R.J."

"What time were you there?"

"What time did they see my car?"

"About 5:15. The park attendant recognized it when she left for the day." He'd eaten his pie in three bites.

"Well, then, that's about the time I was there. I just got the urge late in the day to see the fall leaves and you know, R.J., how much Harmon loved that park. I just found myself there and if they say it was 5:15 then I guess I was there at 5:15."

"Did you see Falkenberry drive up?"

"No, I didn't."

"Did you see anybody suspicious?"

"Just some late tourists. They always look suspicious to me."

We laughed.

"How's your arthritis?" His nod indicated Harmon's cane leaning against my chair.

"Not good. As a matter of fact, it's particularly bad today."

"You ought not to go around looking at leaves on your own, Bonita Faye. You know I'll take you any time you say."

He made like he was fixing to go.

"Wait a minute, R.J. How do they think Baron died? You didn't tell me. Do they think it was an accident?"

"Maybe. Maybe not. Those drug people are rough and he coulda been killed in a drug deal that went sour. Or he coulda heard that we were after him and just plain jumped. After all, he's probably better off dead than where we were going to send him. The Oklahoma City people will look into it, but my guess is that unless somebody confesses, we'll never know."

He got up and nodded at me and then at the manager at the counter. Oklahoma state troopers never have to pay for their pie and coffee at the Black Angus. He was pushing out the front door when I called him back.

"R.J., I reckon Libby must be home from Fayetteville by now. Would you stop by and tell her about Baron?"

A frown wrinkled his brows, but he nodded.

"And would you use the front door? It might scare her if you came in the back this early." I remembered the look of a brown uniform though my lead glass door. I wasn't lookin' for history to repeat itself, but it wouldn't hurt to help it either.

R.J. was almost through the door this time before I called after him again. He patiently returned to my table.

"And, R.J., will you call her 'Elizabeth.' " It was time that girl grew up to the name her mother had given her.

"Can I get you some pie, Miz Adams?" I hadn't seen the waitress at my elbow.

"No, Frances. I think I'm going to go on a diet. The doctor says it will help my arthritis. I'll just have some more coffee, please."

I sat and drank that last cup and thought about what R.J. had told me. If I had waited just one more day, if I had listened more to what R.J. had said about the investigation, if I hadn't thought I had to solve the problem myself. . . . If . . . if . . . if . . . When would I ever learn?

Ain't life funny? Everything was already in the works to take care of my problem, but no, I had to go and kill Baron Falkenberry a day too early.

THIRTY-EIGHT

The doctor was right.

Losing weight did ease the pain in my knees. I was so small boned that carrying around all that extra weight just added to the misery.

I might never have lost as much as I did 'cept for Patsy.

When I got home from the Black Angus that Sunday afternoon, I was so stiff, I couldn't get out of the car. I had to sit and honk until Libby came out and helped me inside. Then she called Patsy.

Libby was red-eyed and her face was blotchy from crying, but all-in-all, I didn't think she was as upset about Baron as she coulda been. She treated me as gentle as a baby as she helped me into bed.

Patsy, however, was a tyrant.

"Bonita Faye Adams, what on earth have you been up to? What have you done to yourself?"

She stood over me, her hands on the broad hips that were the only sign that she had ever borne seven children, and her rosy face that had never seen a lick of

makeup was screwed up as tight as the gray bun she
wore on the top of her head.

"Libby, get me the arthritis ointment and the hot
pads," she ordered.

It was nearly three weeks before Patsy let me get up
to even go in my own kitchen. She and Libby fixed all my
meals, and to tell the truth, I wasn't all that hungry, so
all that low-fat, low-cholesterol food wasn't so bad.

The pounds melted off and the pain and Libby went
away at the same time.

She had decided to go to school in Norman and I wondered, but I didn't ask, if it had anything to do with R.J.
transferring to OSBI in Oklahoma City. If it did, I'd know
someday.

Before she left we had us a little talk.

"I can't thank you enough, Bonita Faye, for all you've
done for me." She put her pretty blonde head over on my
shoulder and started to cry.

"Now, Elizabeth. I've told you and I've told you that I
don't want to hear any more of that."

"But, when I think of how I came here. And how
you've told me so much about my mother. Just when I'd
lost her, I've found her in another way." I'd given the girl
all the mementos I'd kept of her mother's, all but one
tape cassette of a piano recital where Elly had played a
Mozart concerto.

Libby went on. "And Baron Falkenberry. What must
you think of me? R.J. says you understand, but, oh,
Bonita Faye, what a fool I was."

"We all are, Elizabeth, at one time or another over
some man. It doesn't mean you have to carry it around
with you for the rest of your life." She looked up at me
and smiled. She was looking more like Elly every day.

The first night after the girl left, I sat in my rocker in my
living room wrapped in the old afghan. I waited for Harmon, but he never came. "That's all right, Harmon," I

whispered anyway. "I know now that you're dead. You just go on with whatever it is you have to do. And I'll get on with living. I'm sorry I kept you so long." Patsy woulda been mad if she knew I sat in that rocker all night long, sat until the early morning sun shown through my lead glass front door causing colored lights to dance on the living room wall.

"Do you want me to put that in an overhead compartment for you, Mrs. Adams?" The stewardess was trying to help.

"No, I'll hold on to it, but thank you for asking."

"But, it will be almost four hours to Paris, even on the Concorde."

I smiled and said, "I remember when it used to take twelve. It's all right, honey. It's not heavy and I want it close to me."

I looked down at the paper shopping bag that we were arguing over. Sticking up through the thick swaddling of tissue paper was the handle of my orange Fiestaware pitcher. That and my van Gogh postcard were all I'd brought with me that meant anything. And I'd filled the Fiestaware pitcher full of rose petals from my favorite bush when I'd left my little house in Poteau, Oklahoma, for the last time.

As she walked on down the aisle to help another passenger, I wondered what that stewardess had seen when she looked at me. Just a scared, little old gray-haired lady clutching to a misconception of treasure, or a mature woman excited about going on one of the most thrilling adventures of her life.

Probably the old lady, I thought as the space-age plane left the runway. I hadn't been too impressed with what I had seen behind the attendant's eyes that were almost the turquoise blue of Patsy's. "That girl hasn't lived long enough," I said under my breath, but my thoughts were of my best friend that I had left behind.

Patsy had wanted me to go. Had even helped plan my
itinerary and make reservations, but I still hadn't wanted
to leave her until she finally agreed that she'd make her
first trip to France in the spring. "I'd like to be there
when Michel and Sary's first grandchild is born," she'd
said.

So we'd gone on with the plans which were a lot more
thorough and detailed than when I first flew to Paris
over forty years ago.

Although the plane was going to Paris, I wasn't going
to stop there, not even to spend one night with Simone,
Denis, and Robert at the Hotel Regina in Boulogne. They
didn't even know I was coming anyway.

No, I was going to take a sleeper train to Geneva,
Switzerland, and from there, a day coach to Aigle, where
I'd catch the narrow-gauge railroad up to Leysin. Claude
was living there, semi-retired, since Didi's death in a car
accident outside Stockholm two years ago. I hadn't seen
his chateau in Leysin, but he had sent me postcards and
it looked like a mountain village a Heidi would have
loved.

Claude didn't know I was finally ready to come to
him either. For the first time in my life I was going to surprise him.

I carried my shopping bag with me when I went to the
restroom on the plane. While I was washing my hands,
I glanced in the mirror. "Well, hello," I said. My soul was
peeking through today.

When I settled back down in my seat and the Concorde was speeding toward France, I felt like Wonder
Woman at the controls of her invisible airplane. I felt in
charge, but only of my immediate destination.

The glimpse of my soul in the restroom had reassured
me that Billy Roy's death was squared away. If I believed,
I had to believe that.

The other one, the Falkenberry one, still bothered me
some. When I'd asked Baron to meet me at the runestone, was murder on my mind? Had I really wanted to

see the leaves from the higher vista or had I known that a fall from the lower plateau was unlikely to be fatal? Was it premeditated murder or impulse that caused me to shove Baron Falkenberry off that cliff? Did I know that no one was ever going to suspect, much less question, a half-crippled old woman about a death at the end of an extremely physical trail?

Whatever the answers, the results were out of my hands. I remembered what Didi had told me years ago.

"What did you say? Can I help you, Mrs. Adams?" I looked up at the girl with no history in her eyes and shook my head. "No, I'm just talking to myself."

What I hadn't intended to say out loud, but wasn't sorry that I had, was, "Offer it up. I'm tired of being in charge of what comes next. I'll just offer it up."